Bear My Soul

(Fire Bears, Book 1)

T. S. JOYCE

Bear My Soul

ISBN-13: 978-1540755957
ISBN-10: 1540755959

First electronic publication: May 2015

T. S. Joyce
www. tsjoyce.com

NOTE FROM THE AUTHOR:

This book is a work of fiction. The names, characters, places, and incidents are products of the writer's imagination or have been used fictitiously and are not to be construed as real. Any resemblance to persons, living or dead, actual events, locale or organizations is entirely coincidental. The author does not have any control over and does not assume any responsibility for third-party websites or their content.

Published in the United States of America

First digital publication: May 2015
First print publication: December 2016

Editing: Corinne DeMaagd

ONE

Rory Dodson's hands shook as she stacked the papers neatly. This time was going to be different. She wasn't going to let Mr. Farris bully her into staying late. Already, he'd nixed her lunch breaks completely. Out of the entire company, she was the only one who wasn't allowed to take half an hour to eat anymore.

She couldn't tell if the trembling in her hands was from lack of food or worry. She absolutely couldn't be late picking up Aaron. Not again.

She stood, smoothed the wrinkles from her simple black skirt, reminded herself not to roll her ankles in her sky-high heels, and strode around her desk toward the conference room. Mr. Farris had demanded a late meeting today, which never boded well for her leaving on time.

But it was too close to the full moon, and Aaron had been displaying new symptoms lately. If he shifted in a room full of five year olds... *Stop it.* Everything would be fine. Rory was going to set up the meeting so the men wouldn't need her anymore, and then she would slip out, take the back roads through Oklahoma City, and pull into the parking lot right in time with the other moms. She'd been preparing for a smooth meeting all day. This was going to work.

"Ms. Dodson." Mr. Farris greeted her through a humorless, veneer smile. "So nice of you to join us." He made a show of looking at his watch, a piece that probably cost more than her annual salary.

She was a minute early, but already, every seat around the conference table was taken with high-powered men and women in business suits. Determined not to let her boss see how much she hated the way he talked to her in front of everyone, Rory matched his empty smile, then set neatly clipped stacks of paperwork in front of each person. Mathew, the accountant, leaned back in his chair and openly stared at her ass as she bent to settle his stack of notes in front of him. She hated the way he always watched her, as if she was nothing but a slab of meat to judge the marbling in. She repressed a chill as he grinned unapologetically at her—the twit.

After a quick retreat to the side bar as the meeting began, she balanced plates of refreshments on her arms and placed them in the center of the sprawling, oval-shaped table. She could feel Mathew's eyes follow her every move, but she ignored it. Engaging him only gave him a bold tongue and encouraged him to say things that made her skin crawl.

He wasn't anything like Aaron's father.

Just thinking about the stranger brought blazing heat to her cheeks. She turned her back on the room, rested her hand on the handle of the coffee pot, and closed her eyes. Cody Keller. She hadn't seen him since their one night together. No phone calls, no letters—her choice. That man had managed to wreck her heart and give her the best thing that had ever happened to her in one blinding moment. She hated him because he was a stranger who had caused her pain. She loved him because he'd given her Aaron.

And just like any other time she thought of Cody, of his easy smile, warm eyes, and the way his hands had turned gentle with a touch, she was rocked with emotion she didn't understand. Loss and joy, all at once.

If caring about a man hurt like this, she was never, ever going to give her whole heart to anyone.

"Ms. Dodson!" Mr. Farris yelled.

Rory jumped, splashing hot coffee onto the back of her hand. Pain blasted up her nerve endings as she rushed to dry herself off with a napkin and stop the burning.

"We're waiting," Mr. Farris growled.

"Sorry, sir," she rushed out. She needed this job. If she didn't make money, she and Aaron didn't eat.

With a steadying breath, she turned and faced his furious gaze. Mr. Farris's sagging face was red from the thick wrinkles over his throat to his shining, hairless dome. His eyes sparked with something akin to hatred. As she bent at the waist to fill the first coffee mug, Mr. Farris said, "You see, this is why I don't like hiring breeders."

"Breeders, sir?" she asked, hating the word on her tongue.

"Yes. Women who have no drive but to produce needy children, and then slither back into the job market without the time to devote to actual work. And then it's sick days and doctor's appointments and daycare pick-up times. It's a complete tax on all of our time."

Rory dropped her gaze to the two women across the table. One glared at her with vicious contempt that said she couldn't agree more with the vile hate Mr. Farris spewed. The other looked decidedly uncomfortable, but still didn't speak up in Rory's defense. In defense of all women in the work force, really. And maybe that was just as bad as the other woman's agreement with the idea that mothers only belonged in the home, raising their needy children.

"I've already stayed past four o'clock to serve you at this meeting," Rory gritted out.

"If it weren't for HR on my ass about hiring qualified women, I would've gone with literally any other applicant. I mean"—he huffed a laugh and looked around—"how qualified do you have to be to stack paperwork and serve us a fucking cup of coffee? And you can't even do that right!"

Angry heat drove up her neck and landed in the

tips of her ears. She shook with fury as she set the coffee pot on the table by Mathew. She hoped it burned a ring in the mahogany for them to remember her by because this was bowl-sheet, and she was done.

Aaron was probably already searching for her amongst the other moms, and she wasn't there for him. Instead, she was here, being berated by this asshole.

Aaron, Aaron, Aaron. If he shifted before she got to him...

Rory yanked the cordless headset she used to pick up all of Mr. Farris's calls off her head and set it next to the coffee pot. "Someday," she said low, lifting her glare to the two women across the table, "if you decide to have children, you'll look back on this day and feel like absolute rubbish. And you, Mr. Farris. You are a whiskey-belching, conniving, womanizing, disrespectful fuckface!" She strode over to him and dumped his steaming mug over his notes. "It'll be my pleasure to never serve you again. Have a horrible life, trying to make your insignificant existence more bearable by belittling the people around you. Maybe it'll work for you someday." She shot him both fingers and stormed out of the office. "I quit," she screamed over her shoulder just as the door slammed closed.

Huffing a gust of air, she grabbed her purse and a picture of Aaron that sat on her desk, then jogged for the elevator as fast as her heels would let her. She was already late. And now she was jobless. The full weight of what she'd done hit her like a hurricane. She had a little in savings. Hopefully, it would be enough until she could find something else. Maybe she could pick up a job serving tables or something while she was interviewing to supplement the savings. Shit. Rory couldn't believe she'd just done that.

As soon as the elevator doors closed, the angry tears she'd been biting back rained down her cheeks. She couldn't be irresponsible like this. It wasn't only her who was affected by her decisions. Aaron depended on her for everything. He already had things so hard she needed to make things as easy as possible in all the areas of their life she could control.

In the parking garage, it was painfully obvious which car was hers. The ancient Honda hatchback was scratched and scuffed, the fender crooked. The lime green paint job had begun to crack around the door handles, exposing streaks of rust. It was still running like a dream, though, and that was good enough for her. Heels echoing against the concrete, Rory hurried down rows of dark-colored luxury cars—a grating sea of sameness.

She had to try three times to get the key in the lock, on account of her fingers shaking so badly. With a sob, she yanked the door open and turned the engine, then blasted out of the parking spot, squealing her tires. Her epic storm-out was anticlimactic as she had to zigzag her way to the exit, only burning rubber on the straightaways. She screamed and choked the steering wheel.

When she looked down at the time, panic flared in her chest. She was supposed to pick Aaron up from aftercare by 4:10, and it was already five minutes past that.

Aaron used to only shift on full moons, but for the last few months, he'd been showing signs that his inner bear cub was restless, even when the moon wasn't bloated and high in the sky. Aaron's condition was changing, or mutating, or something scientific that she had no guess at because she was no scientist, and she sure as sugar wasn't going to trust anyone by telling them what was going on with him. That little boy was hers. From the day he'd been born, it had been just the two of them against the world.

She would protect him, no matter what.

Rory stomped on the gas and exited the highway as soon as she saw the traffic was already backed up. She couldn't afford to sit there, moving by inches, not knowing what was happening to Aaron.

She pushed the only speed dial number she had saved, and Anna answered. "Rory? Where are you?"

"I'm on my way. Tell him mommy is coming, and he doesn't have to worry about a thing."

"He's..." Static sounded over the speaker, and Anna's voice dipped low. "His eyes, Rory. I don't know what's wrong with him, and you know I've tried to respect your privacy, but I can't hide this from the other teachers anymore. It's too obvious something is wrong."

"Nothing's wrong with him!"

"Just so," Anna said, voice pitched even lower, "I don't think you can do this alone anymore. You need to figure him out or put him in a special program, or...something." Anna inhaled a long breath. "Do you understand what I'm saying to you?"

Defeated, Rory's shoulders slumped as she pulled to a stop at a red light. "You don't think he should go to school there anymore."

"We can talk more about it when you get here. Just...hurry."

Rory ended the call and tossed the cell phone onto the passenger's seat. Tears blurred her vision as she stared at it and gripped the steering wheel. A horn honked from behind her. She wiped her eyes and accelerated through the stale green light.

The preschool was small and attached to the back of a church. Aaron's preschool class was fifteen kids strong. Only a couple of minivans belonging to Anna and one of the other teachers still remained in the parking lot as she pulled in.

Feeling like absolute grit, she ran for the door, nearly twisting her ankle on a misplaced step.

Aaron ran into her arms as soon as she opened the door.

"Hey, baby," she crooned, falling backward. She probably looked ridiculous sitting on the carpet in a skirt with one of her pumps dangling off her toes, but right now, she just needed to hug her kid. Today had been hell.

A tiny snarl rumbled from Aaron's chest, and she stroked his platinum blond hair, a gift from his father. The growl settled, and she eased back and cupped his cheeks. His eyes were fever bright and an odd color—an unnatural mixture of green and gold and certainly not his normal clear blue.

Anna stood against the hallway wall, arms crossed, but her face didn't look combative. Anna looked sad. Rory swallowed hard and hugged Aaron up tight, then gave Anna an understanding smile. Goodbyes were always hard.

"Thank you for being okay with protecting his secret," Rory whispered.

Anna shook her head slowly. "You never let me in on his secret. All I know is that he is a good kid. A sweet one. But this world is going to get ugly on him fast if you don't get help."

"What kind of help?" Rory asked with a frown. Instinctively, she hugged her little man tighter against her chest.

Anna sighed and handed her a piece of paper. It was a drawing done in bright paints with three stick figures in front of a house. In the bottom corner, Aaron had signed his name. Half of the letters had been written backward.

"Did you draw this?" she asked.

Aaron pulled back and smiled at the picture, then nodded.

"And who is this?" she asked, pointing to the smallest figure.

"That's me," he said in his little pipsqueak voice.

"And this one?"

"That's you, momma. Don't you see the eyelashes?"

"I do, baby. But who is this one?"

"That's Daddy Cody."

Rory pursed her lips as her heart broke. She'd given him a picture she and Cody had taken the night they'd spent together. It was the only one she had, and now, it was painfully clear it was the only thing Aaron would ever have of his daddy.

Anna lowered her chin and gave Rory a significant look. "Whatever he's going through, I don't think you can do this on your own."

"But his daddy..." She shrugged helplessly. "We don't know each other, and I don't know if he would understand Aaron's condition. Involving him is a huge risk."

Anna knelt down in front of her, dark hair swishing with the motion. "Rory, I consider you a friend. We've talked often enough, and I know you don't have much support. That's my advice."

"Go get your backpack," Rory whispered, tickling Aaron's ribs.

He giggled and bounded away, clutching the painted picture of a family that could never be.

"What if his father finds out what is happening to Aaron and exposes us?"

"What if he is like Aaron?"

The idea drew her up short. For a while, she'd thought maybe the little bear inside of her son could possibly be genetics, but she'd researched and couldn't find anything on families. All the lore she'd tracked down said shifters were created with a bite from another, so this had to be some sort of evolutionary mutation. Right?

Anna held her hand out and helped Rory up, then hugged her shoulders. Against her ear, she whispered, "It's no longer safe for Aaron here. It takes a village to raise a child, especially one as special as him. You need to find your village." One more squeeze, and the teacher released her.

After Aaron had hugged his teacher goodbye and Rory had buckled him into the back of her junk car, she hesitated starting the engine.

Sound advice. Everything Anna had said rang with this sense of clarity. What if there were more bear shifters like Aaron? What if it wasn't some mistake in his cellular make-up or leap in evolution?

But if she found Cody again, and told him, it meant bringing someone she didn't trust into her inner circle. And at the center of that circle was her baby bear in need of her protection. This decision put him in danger.

But...

Rory leaned her head back against the headrest and looked into the rearview mirror at her son, a smile on his cherry red lips as he sang a song to himself and played with a toy train he'd left in his car seat this morning. His eyes were still the muddy color of something supernatural that dwelled within him.

She couldn't keep him safe like this anymore.

Not alone.

Cody Keller was about to have some very big questions to answer.

TWO

"Are we there yet?" Aaron asked from the back seat.

Rory tossed a smile over her shoulder, relieved that this time, unlike the other eight hundred times he'd asked, she could finally give him the answer he wanted to hear. "Are you ready to meet Aunt Leona?"

"Yes!" he said, fisting his hands around two paperclips he'd found on the floor of the last gas station they'd taken a bathroom break in.

His megawatt smile brought on the nervous flutters that had been assaulting her since her front tires had passed over the Colorado state line. She could still back out of this. She could chicken out, and Cody would never know they were even in town.

That thought settled her churning stomach as she turned onto Harris Street.

Aunt Leona's house hadn't changed one bit since the last time Rory had seen it six years ago. It was still the same color of periwinkle blue with white trim. It had always reminded her of the doll house her father had built her when she was a child. Grass didn't grow very well in Breckenridge because of the altitude, but Aunt Leona had a green thumb that bordered on magical, and she'd somehow got an entire yard of wildflowers and hardy bushes growing in her front yard.

Rory took a deep, steadying breath as she put the car in park. Cody was here in this tiny town…somewhere.

"Come on, little buddy. She's been itching to see you, too," Rory said as she unbuckled Aaron from his car seat.

Aaron grabbed his miniature backpack from the floorboard, then bolted up the gravel path lined with cedar fence posts to keep the wild foliage at bay. Rory laughed despite the nervous tremors that blasted up her spine every time she thought about what she was doing. After tugging the monumentally heavy single suitcase from the car, she shut the hatch back door, settled the luggage on its wheels, and rolled it up the path to Aunt Leona's.

There was a long porch in front with three rocking chairs where her aunt and her two best friends probably watched the joggers and dog walkers who were headed up the street toward the mountain hiking paths. She imagined them giggling and guffawing at the handsome men who passed. Leona always had hilarious stories about Nina and Doris when she and Aaron talked to her on the phone on Saturday evenings.

Aunt Leona was already wrestling the screen door open by the time Rory bumped her luggage up the steps. She was beaming as she bent down and scooped Aaron up in a bear hug.

"You!" she exclaimed. "How are you so big? The last time I saw you, you were a tiny baby."

Aaron giggled, then patted her bouffant hair. "Blue," he observed.

Aunt Leona's grin broadened, and she nodded. "Clever lad. My hair is blue. Do you want to know why?" She offered a wink at Rory over his shoulder. "One of my very best friends said she could dye my hair just the shade it used to be, but when she was finished working on it, it came out this color. Can you believe that?"

Aaron smiled shyly and shook his head.

"Well, I was mad as a hornet and wanted her to change it back immediately, but when she did, it was still this exact color. To make me feel better, my friends, Doris and Nina, dyed their hair the same color. When we went to a town meeting, someone called us the Blue-Haired Ladies, and the name stuck. Byron Crosby even wrote a play just for us to star in over at the local theater called *The Land of Blue-Haired Ladies*. And now the hair has to stay, because people would be sad if there were no Blue-Haired Ladies around anymore. We even got ourselves a float in the Fourth of July parade again this year."

"A float?" Aaron said on a bewildered breath. "What's that?"

"It's a ride with lots of colors. And we get to throw out candy, so if you can beg your mommy to stay through the week, I'll make sure to throw you extra on account of you being the most handsome little man Breckenridge has ever seen. And that's saying somethin', boy, because this town is chalk-ablock full of handsome men." She lifted her chin and leveled him with her happy blue eyes. "Why do you think I've been living here all these years?"

Aaron scrunched up his face. "For handsome men?"

Aunt Leona poked his nose and nodded once. "See? I knew you were a clever lad. Hey, darlin'," she said, pulling Rory in with her free hand and squeezed them both. "I've sure missed you, girl."

And here in Aunt Leona's embrace, Rory could finally admit to herself how blasted much she'd missed her, too. When Aaron had been born, everyone had jumped ship and bailed on her. Everyone except Aunt Leona. It had been way too long since she'd snuggled into one of her aunt's legendary hugs.

When static rang from somewhere in the house, Rory frowned. "What was that?"

"Bulldog One to Alpha Six, do you copy?" A soft voice sounded through the noise.

"Oh!" Leona exclaimed, toting Aaron inside. "That's Doris. She's been tracking..." She looked down at Aaron, then shot Rory a look and mouthed, *Cody*.

Just his name crashed another wave of dread

through her. Aunt Leona picked up a walkie-talkie from the entryway table and pushed the button on the side. "Alpha Six, this is Bulldog One. I have Puma and Baby Cat with me. What's your status?"

"Burly Mancandy is on the move," came the whispered answer.

Burly Mancandy? Rory mouthed through a grin.

She imagined Doris sitting in her old Buick, the one she'd driven years ago, hunched down in the front seat spying on Cody. She had to stop herself from laughing out loud at her imaginings.

Aunt Leona looked terribly serious as she asked, "Where are they going now?"

"It looks like thc whole group is going to eat at the pizzeria."

"Oh, fancy," Aunt Leona said.

"Send Puma on down here. I can't tell if they're getting food to go or not, and I think Burly Mancandy is catching onto me."

"Okay, she's on her way." Aunt Leona tapped the antenna of the radio on her chin and narrowed her eyes at Rory as Doris said, "Copy that. Alpha Six signing off."

Rory pursed her lips so she wouldn't giggle.

"Why don't you just use your cell phones? I hope you didn't buy those radios just for this...mission."

"Stop it with your logic, or you'll suck the fun out of this," Aunt Leona said, leading her into the small bedroom Rory used to stay in when she visited.

Aunt Leona was still carrying Aaron, but settled him on his feet when she reached the door. With a flourish of her hand, she flipped on the light switch and exposed Aaron's dream room. A refurbished bunk bed covered most of the back wall, and by the window was a giant teddy bear chair and shelf of books. Second hand racing cars, all scratched and rusted and perfect for her rambunctious boy, were lined up by the bed, and a painting of a monster truck hung over the dresser.

"Cars!" he yelled, then scrambled toward the toys. Aaron hesitated in front of the trucks, and ran back to Aunt Leona to hug her knees, then handed her one of his two paperclips. "I've been saving this for hours. I have one, too. Now we can match." He showed her the one that still remained pressed against his palm. With a shy smile, he scurried off to play.

Aunt Leona clutched the little treasure to her

chest and looked like she was going to melt into a puddle right then and there. Rory laughed and gave her a side hug, resting her cheek on her shoulder. "I should've brought him to you sooner. I just didn't know how to deal with all the extra stuff here."

"Oh, Rory, don't you worry about that. I knew you'd come back sooner or later. I just had to be patient. I do hope you'll stay for a while, though."

"I've got enough saved up that I can visit for a week. Then we need to get back so I can find work."

"A week," Aunt Leona said with a nod of her head. "We'll make every moment count. Now hurry scurry before Burly Mancandy takes his pizza pie and disappears into the mountains again. We've been tracking his movements all day."

Rory shook her head and huffed a laugh. She shouldn't be surprised that they'd been stalking Cody. Her aunt and friends were as man-crazy as they came.

After freshening up, she slipped into a shirt. One that was *not* covered in the orange chip dust from the snack she'd snarfed down on their way through Denver. Rory checked on Aaron one more time, then hurried out the door before Aaron realized she was gone. Likely, with the way he and Aunt Leona were carrying on with the toy cars, she'd be back before he even noticed her absence.

The pizzeria was right off Main Street and within walking distance. She tightened the lace of her tennis shoe and jogged down the sloping sidewalk toward the main drag in town.

Rory frowned at her beat-up shoes. Perhaps she should've put more thought into what she was wearing to see Cody for the first time. But then again, he probably wouldn't recognize her anyway, seeing as how he'd been inebriated when they'd shared those six hours together all those years ago. Plus, dressing up meant she cared about what he thought about her, and she definitely didn't. Absolutely not.

She had questions.

He hopefully had answers.

That was all.

Even though it was summer, the evenings were still cool enough that she should've brought a hoodie or light jacket. Crossing her arms over her chest, she lengthened her stride and inhaled a draw of fresh mountain air. She'd forgotten how beautiful it was here. The houses that lined the street were tiny

Victorian style homes, many of which had been kit homes built in the 1800s when the gold mining town had first flourished. Down below, she could make out the tops of the buildings that lined Main Street, and back behind her were piney mountain passes where tourists and townies alike enjoyed hiking and biking. The sun was already half set over the trees. She'd loved it here as a kid. Hell, she loved it still, despite her unfortunate decisions when she'd been a wild-child twenty-year-old.

Rory smelled the high-end pizzeria before she saw it. The ski town was a hub of unique dining, but this place had always been one of her favorites to eat at during her childhood visits. It was tiny, seating only twenty or so at a time in cramped quarters, but the food and ambiance couldn't be beat.

She rushed inside before she could change her mind and looked around. It was busy, and there was a wait in the small entryway, but she spied Cody immediately and was rocked back on her heels by how much he'd changed and how little, all at once.

He sat by a girl, surrounded by friends. He laughed at something the striking brunette said, then took a sip of water as he listened to the man across the table. His hair was shorter than he'd worn it before, but still obviously blond. He kept his waves a little longer on top, and his eyes were still so light in color they were baby blue in the dim lighting. His face looked just the same as she remembered. Strong nose, chiseled jaw, dimples when he smiled deeply enough. What she hadn't expected was for him to be so muscled up. His arms fought against the thin fabric of the long-sleeved shirt he wore, and his neck looked strong enough that he could probably smash a pecan between his chin and chest. His fingers were graceful, though, as he traced condensation across the bottom curve of his water glass. The girl beside him whispered something into his ear. He stared vacantly ahead, his eyes filled with a faraway look as she spoke. He was practically looking at Rory, but apparently saw right through her, as if his mind was in outer space. As the brunette giggled against his neck, Rory stood frozen in the doorway.

"'Scuse me," a man said as he sidled around her, "are you in line?" He pointed to the counter beside her.

"Oh, no. Yes. Yes, I'm in line. To buy pizza. Because that's what you do here."

The man frowned and canted his head. “Great.”

She couldn’t do this.

She couldn’t just walk over to Cody’s table when he was obviously with someone. What was she going to say? All those hours and miles in the car on the way from Oklahoma, and had she given a single fleeting thought to how she would broach the subject of his surprise child? No. She’d drowned her worries in cheese puffs and blared kiddie songs on a deafening level while Aaron slept like a stone most of the trip here.

This had been a terrible idea. Worse than terrible. Cody had a life now and couldn’t be trusted to keep Aaron’s secret. No. Nope, nope, nope.

Wuss that she was, she ordered a pie and hid in the corner behind a man in a giant cowboy hat while she waited for her order to be ready. And try as she might, she couldn’t keep her eyes away from Cody. It was uncanny how much Aaron looked like him. She’d meant to tell him about his son in person after she’d figured everything out. But then Aaron had shifted for the first time, and she’d realized she was truly alone in the world if she was to keep her baby safe.

Not even Aunt Leona knew what was sleeping

inside of her boy.

Rory would bring the pizza home for dinner and tell Aunt Leona she'd changed her mind. She would enjoy the week, avoid Aaron's father, and spend time with her aunt until it was time to go back to reality and find work. Yes, that was what she'd do. Good plan.

Or it was a good plan until Cody's nostrils flared and his head jerked up, eyes landing directly on her before she was able to squeak and hide behind the cowboy beside her again.

He probably didn't see her. And even if he had, he definitely wouldn't recognize her. If she just squeezed her eyes tight enough, she could convince herself she was safe in this little corner.

"I know you," a deep voice said.

Rory cracked her eye open to see Cody standing right in front of her. He seemed to take up much more space than he actually did, and she wasn't the only one who'd noticed because Cowboy Hat had skedaddled. "Nope, I'm certain you don't."

Cody narrowed those gorgeous baby blues and nodded slowly. His smile was uncertain, as if he thought she was playing a game with him. "Yeah, I do.

You're Rory."

"Puma!" the cashier yelled out.

Rory offered him a too bright smile and ducked around him. Geez, he was a giant. She had to journey around his massive shoulders to get to the register.

"Puma?" he asked.

Damn skippy! She was way too intelligent to use her real name. She paid for the pizza and gave a little flutter of her fingers until Cody moved out of the way, then stepped through the door and out into the cool night air.

"What are you doing here?" he asked from right behind her.

Closing her eyes, she inhaled deeply, psyching herself up to face the man she'd been scared of ever since she realized he could have a permanent stake in her life.

"I'm visiting family," she murmured, opening her eyes and turning around. She came face to nipples with his barrel chest. Arching her neck, she looked up into his curious gaze. Holy mayo, she'd bred with a Titan.

Gripping the pizza, she asked, "I also wanted to ask you something."

"Yeah, sure," he said, his eyebrows drawing down in concern. "Shoot. Ask me anything."

"Is there something you..." Shit, how did she word this so that she could back out of the conversation easily? "Do you have anything strange or maybe supernatural in your medical history?"

Cody's face went comically blank.

A knocking on the pizzeria window pane sounded, and they both turned. The girl he'd been sitting next to, the pretty brunette with glossy pink lips and an impatient quirk to her dark eyebrows, held up her hands in a *what-the-hell* gesture.

"I'll be right in," he said, as if she could hear him through the glass. Turning to Rory, he leaned down and asked, "What are you talking about? Supernatural what? Like ghosts?"

He did look truly baffled, and clearly, she'd been right in the first place that he didn't know anything about people shifting into bears, but she had to know for sure. She was in the thick of it now, so she might as well be thorough before she slunk back into oblivion. "There's nothing special about you? No superpowers or anything?"

He straightened his spine and crossed his arms

over his chest. A defensive posture if she'd ever seen one, but that was fine. She was using the pizza box as a shield to keep a safe distance between them.

"No, Rory. I don't have any superpowers. Is this some kind of joke?" He looked around suspiciously. "Are you videotaping this or something? Because I have to tell you, I've been followed around by two little old ladies all day, and now you come back after, what has it been? Six years? The whole day has felt weird."

"Of course I'm not videotaping," she rushed out, utterly frustrated at the dead end she'd found. He was obviously not a bear shifter like Aaron, and now she'd wasted both of their time. "Well, it was lovely to see you again, Cody, but my pizza is getting cold and your girlfriend looks pissed. I'll see you around."

She turned and walked away, and this time, thankfully, Cody didn't follow her.

Just as well. What good was rekindling any kind of friendship with the man if he was a risk to Aaron's secret?

THREE

Stupid tears.

Stupid tears and stupid emotions.

Cody had looked damned good, and now Rory's feelings were all mixed up. He was the father of her child, and she'd always cared for him, a complete stranger. Damn him for tethering her heart to him. She couldn't look at Aaron without remembering Cody and that night. And now, after seeing him again, she'd have to go through the mourning process all over again. She used to imagine having this perfect family. She'd made up personality traits she admired in him, and when she'd taken Aaron out to the park or to the movies, she'd always imagined what it would be like if Cody was there. Which was stupid because she didn't even know him.

She settled the pizza on one of the rocking chairs on Aunt Leona's front porch so she could wipe her eyes and plaster on a happy smile. It wouldn't do anyone any good for Aaron to get upset. Not until she had the cage set up somewhere safe and private.

Thinking about the cage brought on another wave of grief. It was a ridiculous notion, but she'd hoped that Cody would somehow help her figure out a way not to cage her son during his Changes anymore.

Dammit! She sagged into a rocking chair as her shoulders slumped under the defeat. She'd been silly, wishing that Cody would just magically understand what she needed and come to her rescue. That wasn't what happened in the real world. Men didn't do stuff like that. All of her hopes of Cody being able to help her with Aaron—and the tiny bear that sat waiting just under his skin—were dashed the second his face went blank in confusion. He wasn't like Aaron. He couldn't be part of this. She was back to being all alone and scared for her child's future.

The blow was crushing.

She sobbed as quietly as she could, leaned over

her knees with her arms gripped around her stomach. Dark now, it felt safer outside than inside with her aunt and son to witness her breakdown.

"She isn't my girlfriend," Cody said, breaking the blissful silence of the night.

Rory jerked her head up and gasped, then wiped her eyes furiously. "I'm not crying because you have a girlfriend. This isn't even about you."

"Bullshit. I can hear the lie in your voice." The chair beside her creaked under his weight as he sank down onto the worn rocking chair.

"How did you find me?" she asked.

"I followed you. I have something to say. Something I wish I could've said a long time ago, but when I woke up after we were together, you were just gone. I looked for you," he admitted low, elbows on his knees and hands clasped in front of him. "I thought it would be easy to track you down because the name Rory isn't that common, but I came up empty."

Afraid the lump in her throat would make her voice sound strange, she nodded and snuck a glance at his rigid profile. He was angry.

"You know, you don't always have to run away,"

he said, swinging his gaze to her. "Even if things get tough, sometimes it could be worth it to stick around."

"I had a reason for running, Cody."

"Which was?"

It didn't feel right telling him everything. Not when she didn't trust him, but she could give him something. "You said her name when we were together."

Cody's eyes flashed, and he leaned back into the chair, studying her. "Whose name?"

"Sarah's. You whispered it right at the end." Mortification burned her cheeks, and she dropped her gaze to the toes of her tennis shoes. "Right when we were finishing. I thought you had been there with me. I know that sounds stupid, but I liked you. It was this instant gravitational pull to you, but you hadn't really been there with me. You were thinking of her. Of Sarah. I didn't want to be some woman's replacement for the night. Obviously, you still loved her. I didn't run, Cody. I bowed out of a race I couldn't win."

Cody scrubbed his oversize hands down his face, and when he looked at her again, he looked exhausted or devastated, or perhaps both. "Sarah was part of the reason I wanted to talk to you. She was the reason I tried so hard to find you again. You saved me from an awful fate, Rory. I'd bonded to this girl, Sarah, when I was young. Too young maybe, but it wasn't in my control."

"Bonded?"

"It's like...it's like being in love, but harder."

"Harder how?"

"It's nearly impossible to fall out of that kind of devotion, even if the person you've bonded to isn't healthy for you. All I could see for the longest time was her, and then you came along. One night with you, and everything was clear again. I was able to let her go because of you. I wanted to thank you. In this insane way that I have no power to explain to you, you saved me that night." Cody shrugged, as if his tight-fitting thermal sweater was growing uncomfortable. "So...thank you, Rory I-Never-Figured-Out-What-Your-Last-Name-Was."

She huffed a soft laugh and said, "Dodson. My last name is Dodson."

"Dodson," he repeated in a quiet voice.

The porch light flipped on, illuminating what was

probably a serious case of raccoon eyes and twin mascara rivers running down her cheeks. But above the panic of how zombie-like she must look was the realization that the door was opening.

"No!" she yelled. Too late.

Aunt Leona's eyes went wide as she looked at Rory, then Cody, just as Aaron ran past her legs.

"Oh dear," her aunt said as Aaron skidded to a stop with a grin on his face.

"We're going to check the mail and look for lizards and fireflies. Is that pizza?"

Rory had frozen under the avalanche of shock. She'd led Cody—human, untrustworthy Cody—right to her son. She could feel him staring over her shoulder, and her heart lurched at what he must be seeing right now. Platinum blond hair, blue eyes, and dimples that matched his own.

Aaron's gaze drifted from her face to just above her shoulder, and his smile faltered. He shrunk back toward Aunt Leona's legs, then squinted. "Daddy Cody?"

Shee-yit.

Rory dared a glance at Cody. The blood had drained from his face entirely, leaving him pale as a phantom, mouth hanging slightly open as his chest heaved against the tight fabric of his sweater. His clear blue eyes shifted to hers in an accusatory glare. "Does he bear my mark?"

Rory shook her head, baffled. "I don't know what that means."

"This," he said through clenched teeth. He pulled at the collar of his shirt and exposed a light brown birthmark.

Her heart pounded, and a tiny shocked sound squelched from her throat. It was bigger than Aaron's, but the exact same shape. It looked like a strawberry.

"Rory," he said as a muscle under his eye twitched, "tell me now." His eyes had gone wide, and his words quaked.

"Baby, come here." She held out her arms as Aaron walked toward her, then cuddled him up in her lap. With a deep inhalation, she pulled back the collar of his blue striped sweater, exposing the miniature mark.

Cody's face went utterly blank as he stared at it. Moments dragged on, and Aaron began to fidget.

The boy turned in her lap and handed Cody the

paperclip he was still clutching. "I gave my other one to Aunt Leona, but you can have mine."

Life filtered back into Cody's eyes as he lowered his gaze to the paperclip nestled against Aaron's tiny palm. "Thank you," he said on a breath, taking the gift. "What's your name?" His voice had gone deep and emotional.

"Aaron Daniel Dodson." He smiled and snuggled against Rory, wrapping his slender arms around her neck.

"That's a fine name. I'm Cody Leland Keller."

"Leland?" Aaron asked, his tiny nose scrunched.

"It's a family name. My brothers have the same middle names, too. Kind of strange, huh?"

Aaron nodded. "Are you here to eat some of our pizza?"

Cody huffed a laugh and shook his head. "I came to speak with Rory—I mean, with your mother."

Aaron looked at the pizza box, then back to Cody, and shrugged his shoulders up to his ears. "Will you?"

Cody shook his head and let off a sigh. "Buddy, I don't... That's up to your mom."

"I'm off to dinner with the Blue-Haired Ladies," Aunt Leona announced as she flounced down the steps, purse in hand. "Don't wait up. We old ladies get wild and crazy on Friday nights."

Cody narrowed his eyes at Aunt Leona's receding back. "Are you the ones who've been following me around town all day?"

Apparently, Aunt Leona didn't hear him, or didn't want to, because she didn't even miss a step as she disappeared into the dark.

"He's into sharing," Rory explained as Aaron opened the box and looked in wide-eyed wonder at the meat lover's pie. "That's what they've been learning at preschool. And he's really very sweet about it. I guess what I'm saying is, we would love for you to eat with us."

"Yeah, you look like you could eat a whole pizza by yourself, Daddy Cody!"

"Aaron," Rory warned, shaking her head. "I think you should just call him Cody. That might make him more comfortable."

Aaron's face fell. "Why?"

Cody gave the boy a troubled look and rubbed his hand roughly through his cropped, blond hair. "You have him in preschool? The public kind?"

"Of course. He's five. He'll be in kindergarten

next year, and he needed to learn how to mind his teachers, stand in lines, share, and work well with the other kids. Plus, I have to work for both of us. He goes to school while I work."

He frowned at the back of her son's head as Aaron made his way down to the walkway, pizza slice in hand. "Has he Changed yet?"

Warning bells slammed against the inside of her head as she froze. "I don't know what you mean," she said carefully.

"Yeah, you do, or you wouldn't have been asking me about my supernatural family history."

Instead of answering, she crossed her arms over her stomach and watched Aaron move tufts of bushes aside, probably in search of the lizards Aunt Leona had told him about.

"Look at me," Cody said in a soft, deep voice.

She slid her gaze to him and gasped. His eyes were the same muddy, golden green that Aaron's turned to when he was upset, or on the verge of a Change.

He held her in his feral gaze. "When?"

Her breath trembled as she struggled to draw air into her lungs. This was it. This was the moment when she let another soul in on their secret, and he was a stranger. She closed her eyes, bolstering her bravery before she whispered, "He Changed for the first time when he was one."

"Shit," Cody murmured, covering his face with his hands, then flinging them away. "Rory, why didn't you tell me? Why didn't you come to me about him? I have a *kid*, and you left me out of his life completely."

"I meant to tell you," she whispered, tears stinging her eyes at the memory. "I'd bought plane tickets to come back and let you meet him. He'd just turned one, and I was nervous about flying with a baby, but I did all this research and had this plan to come here anyway during winter break. I was still trying to finish college then. But then he Changed, and I knew if you weren't like him, and you found out, you would put him in danger—tell someone or report him to the police or something. And I didn't know anything about what was happening to him. I did research, but all the public library had was lore and myth. Nothing concrete that told me how to help my child through this awful thing he was going through."

"It isn't awful."

"It is for us! He cries and cries around each

Change, and it looks so painful. I listen to my baby's bones break every month. And when he got bigger and his canines came in, I couldn't comfort him anymore. He turns wild." She shoved her arm at him and rolled it over to expose the long scars across her forearm.

Cody's fingers were warm and steady as he slid them down the length of the long-healed claw marks. He dropped her arm and stared at his hands as if he hadn't given them permission to touch her. Her skin turned cold where his warm fingers had been. Confused at the wash of emotion surging through her at his touch, she wrapped her arms around her stomach and covered the scars.

"What did you do?"

"I built him a cage. Our lives are consumed by when his next Change will be. It used to only be around the full moon, but now he shows symptoms more often, and I don't know what to do. I need help."

"That's why you've come back?"

She nodded once.

"It's not supposed to be like that," he rasped out. "He can't be caged, or his animal will grow aggressive and angry." Cody cut her a pleading look. "You need him to grow into a man who can control the animal inside of him."

Her face crumpled as the moisture that had been rimming her eyes spilled over. Embarrassed, she wiped her lashes and clenched her fists in her lap. "I know. I can see him getting worse, but I have no tools to help him."

"Shhh," Cody hushed her. "Everything will be okay. We'll figure this out."

"Are you mad at me?" she asked. It suddenly mattered if he hated her.

"Yeah. I have a son, and I missed all of his life until now. That was your choice. I'm mad as hell, but reaming you out isn't going to fix what's been done." A soft rumbling noise rattled from his chest. His eyes were still feral, and though he was trying to be soft with her, his fists were clenched like hers were.

She'd done this.

"I think I should go," he said in a low, gravelly voice. "This is a lot, and I'm confused. If Aaron can't control his Changes yet, he doesn't need to be around what's going on inside of me." Cody stood and turned at the porch stairs. "Don't run this time, Rory. I won't stop until I find you. He's mine, too." His eyes were hard as he descended the stairs.

Rory stood and rushed to the railing. "I'm really sorry." Her voice was thick with emotion, but hang it. She'd had her reasons for keeping Aaron to herself. She'd wanted to keep him safe, but the hurt look on Cody's face was heartbreaking.

"Don't," he gritted out. He hesitated by Aaron and squatted down, his powerful legs folding beneath him. "I've got some stuff to do, but I'll see you later, okay?"

Aaron nodded, his eyes sad and the corners of his little lips turned down as if he expected to never see Cody again. Maybe he wouldn't. Rory didn't know. Maybe this was too much and Cody would be the one running this time. She imagined lots of surprised fathers in this situation would do the same.

"Thanks for the paperclip, buddy." Cody squeezed Aaron's frail shoulders with his oversize hand, then stood and left without another glance back at her.

She'd earned that—his anger.

Rory had been so focused on keeping Aaron safe she'd never considered that Cody might want to be in his life despite the animal inside of their son. She'd let all the reasons not to tell Cody pile up until it seemed like the only decision a good and protective mother could make.

But Cody was right. He'd missed all of the baby years because of her need to hide Aaron away. And the consequences of his hurt and anger were on her.

Rory wouldn't blame him if he ran.

She deserved nothing less.

FOUR

Cody fingered the tiny paperclip Aaron had given him and tried to tune out the droning weatherman on the television above the bar.

Five fucking years, and she just now came back? And with a kid—his kid. The strawberry-shaped mark on his shoulder blade was the freaking Keller crest. There was no denying Aaron was his.

He'd been sitting here for two hours trying to wrap his head around the reasons she'd kept Aaron a secret. Human or no, Rory had protective momma bear written all over her. It was clear she'd been trying to keep her boy safe in case Cody wasn't a shifter like Aaron, but it still stung something fierce to be left out of the kid's entire life. He'd missed everything. Every milestone. Every late night feeding and scraped knee. First steps, first words, first tooth...

Her supernatural question at the pizzeria had thrown him hard. Of all the times he'd imagined running into her again, he hadn't ever fantasized about her asking if he was harboring a damned grizzly in his gut. He would've broken that little gem to her gently if she'd have stuck around long enough the first time.

He'd liked her. More than liked her, but now things were different. He'd changed in the years they'd spent apart and now wanted no part of any kind of relationship with a woman. Taking Shayna out had been a way to get Ma off his back about moving on from the broken bond with Sarah.

He tilted the bottle and took a long swig. Up to his eyeballs in women problems, and he hadn't dated a damned one in years.

A familiar scent hit his nose, and he slid a nonplussed glare at the door where his older brother, Gage, stood. He got his height and blond hair from Ma's side of the family, but Gage's coffee dark eyes were all Dad's. Cody shoved the paperclip deep in his pocket. Maybe if he ignored Gage, his brother would get the hint and shove off. He wasn't in the mood to talk right now.

Gage took the bar seat next to him. "Shayna's worried."

"Yeah, I could tell from the thirty-seven calls I've ignored from her. Piss off, Gage. I have some shit to sort out."

"Yeah, and you also have a forty-eight hour shift starting in the morning, and you're at a bar drinking by yourself, which I've seen you do exactly zero times before now." He jerked his chin at Cody's beverage and told the bartender he'd "have one of those."

Cody leaned back in the bar chair, growing more irritated by the moment. "What do you want?"

"That was her, wasn't it? At the pizzeria. That was Rory."

"You want a detective's badge?"

"Ma sent me. That's why I'm here."

"You told Ma?" Prick.

"You can't blame me for that one. Boone called her before we even left the restaurant. You know, the timing on this sucks."

"You don't know the half of it."

"Well then explain it, brother. Because I've never seen you get worked up over a woman like this. Not since Sarah. And you finally asked Shayna out—"

"Hold on, now that's not fair. Shayna's been relentless for two years, and you boys weren't helping. And Ma… Look, I'm not interested in another bond. I don't get why you don't understand that. Boone and Dade don't want a bond, and no one gives them shit over it. But with me, you push and push until I take a girl out I'm not interested in. Even if it was a group thing, I don't like being forced into a pairing."

Gage thanked the bartender when he set the beer in front of him and took a long pull of his drink. "We push you because it's different for you. You're the alpha. You should be paired up. You're twenty-eight now, Cody. I get that you were burned by Sarah, but fate got you out of that. Fate and Rory. You have a second chance to find someone worth the risk."

"It's different for you, Gage. You found Leah. Your bond has always been healthy. Both of you are devoted. Sometimes it doesn't work like that."

"So you'll just go your whole life alone. I know you look down on my life. You think I've sold out for mating Leah and having cubs—"

"No, brother," Cody said with a humorless laugh. He shook his head and drained the beer. "I always envied you and Leah, and the cubs. I love your family. I've watched you for years, wishing Sarah had been half the woman Leah was. Even half, and we could've worked without her shredding me. It's not that I don't want a family. I just never, ever want the bond again."

"Is that why you're torn up about Rory being back?"

Leaning forward on his elbows against the sticky bar top, Cody sighed. "I can't have Rory."

Gage shrugged his shoulders up to his earlobes with a baffled expression. "Why not? You could have any lady in this town. In this county, if you wanted. I didn't see a ring on her finger tonight. I know because I looked."

"She has a kid, Gage," Cody blurted out. Gritting his teeth, he closed his eyes and murmured, "She had *my* kid."

"Shit," Gage murmured.

"Shit, indeed."

"Is he marked?"

"Yeah. Same place as me even. If you saw him, you wouldn't question it. He's mine."

"A boy? A son?"

The word *son* sounded strangely exciting in a way that confused the piss out of Cody. He frowned down at his beer and nodded his head.

Gage gripped his shoulder and shook him slowly. "You're a dad?"

More fluttering in his stomach. Maybe it was nausea. *Dad.*

"Wait, okay." Gage linked his fingers behind his head and leaned back until he was staring at the ceiling with a stupid grin on his face. "Okay."

"You said that already."

"Shut up, man. This is blowing my mind right now. What does he look like?"

Cody snorted. "Like a Keller. Towheaded. He looks just like the pictures of me at that age."

Gage beamed—*beamed,* the ass. Like this was anywhere close to the ideal way of becoming a father. "You marked him up good, didn't you?"

"Are you congratulating me for my fifteen minutes of help with him? Seriously?"

"Hell yeah, I am. Being a father is... Cody, your

life is about to change in the coolest ways."

"Yeah, except you forgot one thing. I'm not with Rory. She left me out of his life completely until tonight. She didn't come back here because she has long buried feelings for me. She came back because she needs help with Aaron."

"Aaron," Gage whispered, the dumb smile spreading his face like he hadn't just heard what Cody had said.

"Forget it, man," Cody grumbled, throwing enough cash on the bar to cover the beer and a nice tip. "I can't talk about this with you."

"Why not?"

"Because I need you to have my back. I need you to just listen and sympathize. I'm not like you, Gage. I'm not a family man. I just found out I have a kid. A kid. A five-year-old, intelligent, sweet kid that hasn't needed anything from me his whole life."

"So, you can make it up to him. Rory is here because she needs you in her son's life, right?"

"*Our* son. Yeah."

"I get why you feel like you can't go after Rory, and that sucks. You can't screw up a relationship with your kid's mother. Especially if she's a runner. But

Aaron has a chance to thrive here with cousins his own age and a family. This isn't the end of your life, Cody. It's the beginning of it."

"Krueger is back." Just thinking of the government official that made his life a living hell, Cody fought the urge to grip the bottle until it shattered in his hands.

"What?" Gage asked, leaning forward and pitching his voice low. "How long?"

"He's been pressing on me for two months. I think he's prepping me for another mission or maybe another tour. I don't know."

"Why didn't you tell us?"

"Because that's the burden of the alpha sometimes, brother. He threatens exposure, threatens my family, and I do whatever he wants me to."

Gage's eyes rolled closed, and he rubbed his forehead. "You're worried he'll find out about Aaron."

Defeated, Cody nodded. "If I pursue a relationship with my kid, I put both him and his mother in danger. And she's human, Gage. She's not built to survive the shit we've lived through. She was afraid to let me know Aaron existed because she thought I'd be a danger to him." The words he needed to say bubbled like acid up his throat. "She's right."

For the last four years, Krueger had been the middle man between the Breck Crew and a government bent on using them for their unique abilities. Two tours in the war and several black ops missions Cody wasn't allowed to talk about, and it was clear as crystal the government was just getting started with him and his brothers. Oh, they knew exactly who and what the bears of Breckenridge were. Each of the Breck Crew sported a tracker in their neck to make sure they were neatly controlled and watched by Big Brother. And now Aaron would be in the crosshairs, too.

"What is the threat this time?" Gage asked in a somber tone.

"They're considering making us register as shifters to the public."

"They're going to out us?"

"Not if I do what they say. That's the current deal, anyway."

Gage made a single clicking sound behind his teeth and looked sick. "They won't stop until you're dead, Cody."

He cracked his knuckles and stared over the glass case of fine whiskeys behind the bar. "I know."

He'd accepted that years ago, but now he had something else to fight for besides his crew. Besides his family.

He had a son. And he couldn't stand the thought that someday, when he was a casualty of what the agency forced him to do, Krueger would press on Aaron the same way.

FIVE

Cody had definitely bowed out.

It had been two days since he'd met Aaron, and Rory hadn't seen hide nor hair of him since.

Her boy had asked where he was, and at a loss for what to tell him, she did her best to keep him happy and distracted. Aunt Leona had helped by filling their days with fun. They'd painted pottery at a little shop at the base of the mountain, and it would be ready, fired, and usable in another couple of days when the nice lady who worked there pulled the soup bowls they'd painted out of the kiln. They'd gone on hikes and visited a dog park so Aaron could watch the puppies play. And at the river that wound right along Main Street, they'd watched the brown backs of trout as they waited for tourists to throw pellets of food down to them. Aunt Leona had even taken them on a special tour of a gold mine up the mountain where Aaron got to pan for little flakes. Ever since he'd been carrying the little vial with a smattering of tiny gold flecks inside. A trio of miniature donkeys had followed them around the mine, waiting for them to share the snacks they'd brought.

Rory felt relaxed for the first time in as long as she could remember. She'd hadn't had a vacation or even a day to just be since Aaron had been born. It was easier here, lighter. Aunt Leona truly loved her great nephew and helped watch him so Rory could relax and look around every once in a while.

And Breckenridge was stunning in the summer. Lush greens covered everything, and in every piney wilderness they hiked through, frogs croaked and bees hummed. This had been her paradise growing up. Visiting her aunt on summer breaks from school had always been what she waited for all year. She'd gotten bogged down in her fog of worry since she'd become a mother, but now, she was reminded of just how much she loved this place. For the first time in a long time, she could enjoy Aaron's playful spirit.

His peals of laughter were a balm to her soul and took the sting off Cody's rejection.

But in the quiet moments, like when she was sitting on a boulder watching her son wade in the shallows of the trout river, or when she reclined on a bench as he skipped around the playground off Main Street, or right now, as she washed the dinner dishes—that's when she thought of Cody.

Why had he acted hurt if he had no intention of seeing his son again? Why had he told her not to leave if he wasn't going to make the effort to connect with Aaron? She'd gotten a glimpse that he cared, but maybe she'd been mistaken.

The phone rang as she rinsed a plate. Rory smiled to herself because it was probably Nina or Doris, who phoned frequently. Aaron was bathed and in his little plaid moose pajamas, ramming two trucks together on the wooden floor beside her as she cleaned up from the homemade lasagna dinner she'd made for the three of them.

"Hey," Aunt Leona said low. "This call's for you."

Frowning, Rory rinsed the suds off her hands and dried them, then took the cordless landline from her aunt. "Hello?"

"Hey, it's me." Oh, what Cody's voice did to her insides, all deep and husky like that.

She patted Aaron's head, then stepped into the other room. "I thought you forgot about us."

"Ha, no. You guys are all I can think about, actually. I'm sorry it took so long for me to get back with you. I should've told you. I'm on a forty-eight hour shift up at the station."

"Station?"

"Yeah, I'm a firefighter. I do two days on, three days off. Listen, I was wondering if I could drop by after I get off in the morning. How early do you wake up?"

Rory sank down onto the bottom bunk in Aaron's room and stared at the rails above her. "What time would I like to wake up? Noon, but Aaron wakes up with the birds."

Cody chuckled and said, "He's a morning person?"

"Yeah. You should hear him when he wakes up, too. There is no grumpy phase with him. He chatters on and on about any and everything. His good moods are borderline obnoxious that early," she teased. "So, a firefighter, huh? That sounds like a dangerous profession."

"You worried about me?"

She inhaled sharply at the turn the conversation had taken.

"Sorry," he muttered. "This is uncharted territory for me. So…I've been thinking."

"That sounds foreboding."

"I think we should come up with some ground rules. Together. We don't know each other very well, and now we have a kid together. Or we've always had a kid together, but now I have to figure out where I belong in this family, you know?"

"Family?" she whispered.

"Yeah, Rory. I'm not asking you to fall in love with me, but I think we have to form some kind of friendship in order for this to work so we can both have a relationship with Aaron and it be as easy as possible for everyone."

"So, you want to be friends?"

"Yes. Just friends. You can date whomever you want, and I'll do the same. It'll take the pressure off of us."

Date other people. Her mind was absolutely not on dating right now, but if she was being honest, she didn't like the thought of Cody with anyone else. Wait, what? Where had that troubling thought come from?

"Okay, you'll continue dating that woman you were with at the pizzeria." She could do this—be mature about having a friendship with Aaron's father.

"Okay, now you go," he said.

"Hmm?"

"What are your rules? I know you have them with Aaron. Lay 'em on me."

"Oh, right. Okay, no overnight visits or alone visits until I'm comfortable."

"You mean until you trust me," he said in a flat voice.

"Yes. And just to be up front, I'm only staying through the rest of the week, so I might not get there on this trip."

The other end went silent.

"Cody? Are you still there?"

"Yeah." His voice cracked, and he cleared his throat. "I just didn't realize you'd be taking him away so soon. Okay, but you'll visit. How often?"

"As often as I'm able if it'll help Aaron. And if you want the relationship. With him," she added. "I just left my job, though, and need to find work after this week, so I don't know how long it will be between this visit and the next one. I don't know how much vacation time I'll be allowed off, and we live far away. It gets expensive, and well, I don't have much money. Not that I'm asking for any. We do fine, but it's just been Aaron and me for a long time."

"Where do you live?"

"Oklahoma."

"Jesus," he murmured, sounding a lot less happy than he had a few minutes ago. "If it's money that is ever the problem keeping you from here, please tell me. I'll take care of it."

"I don't feel right about that."

"You don't have to feel right about it, Rory. Aaron is my kid, too, and I haven't paid for anything his whole life. If you ever need help, tell me, and I'll take care of you. I mean...you, as in both of you. Geez, I've been thinking about this conversation for two days, and I meant to be smoother about it."

Her eyebrows wrenched up as she pursed her lips. Cody was about seven levels out of her league, and he was nervous about talking to her? "I think you are being very smooth."

"You're teasing me."

"We're friends, right? Teasing comes along with the territory."

He inhaled deeply across the line. "I get off at seven in the morning. Can I take you and Aaron out for breakfast? There's this donut place on the main strip that serves giant pancakes. I don't want to put too much on you too fast, but my family wants to meet you and Aaron."

"Your family?" Nervous flutters filled her stomach, and she rolled to her side on the bed. "Tomorrow?"

"If I don't let them meet you, my Ma will be up at your aunt's house begging a visit with her grandson. She's been like a dog on a bone since you blew into town."

"Whoa, I just realized Aaron has a grandma. That's crazy."

"Are your parents not in the picture?"

"Umm." None of her wanted to have this conversation now, or ever, really.

"It's okay if you don't want to talk about it."

"I don't. Not yet," she said softly, grateful that he was giving her an out. A subject change was best. "So, are you at the fire station right now?"

"Yeah. We have our own bedrooms up here. Nothing fancy, just a small room with a bed, closet, and an outlet to charge my phone. Which reminds me. Most of the time, we stay pretty busy up here, but if you need me, try to call my cell. If I don't pick up right away, I'll call you back as soon as I can. I mean, if Aaron is Changing and you need help, or if you just want to talk. About Aaron. Or anything. Just call." He cleared his throat again. "Is the boy still up?"

"Yeah. His bath time is around eight every night. Aunt Leona bought him these red and black plaid long-john pajamas that say *Moose Caboose* on the little butt-flap. They're so cute, it's ridiculous." God, the longer she talked to Cody, the easier this felt. It was nice to share this stuff with someone who didn't just have to *ooh* and *aah* out of politeness, but with a person who actually had a stake in her son's life.

"Would you mind if I talk to him for a minute?"

Cody sounded so shy asking that question, it melted her heart into a little puddle. "Yeah," she said, a little choked up. "Let me go get him."

Back in the kitchen, she handed Aaron the phone, and his eyes lit up like firecrackers when she told him it was Cody. She couldn't hear the other side of the conversation, but the minute Cody had asked for turned into lots of minutes as Aaron told him all about the adventures they'd been on over the past two days. It was cute to hear his take on it. His stories tended to circle back to a frog he almost caught, and she giggled frequently as she led him into the bedroom and tucked him in while he chattered away.

"Can you sing me a lullaby? Mommy's tucking me in, and she always sings. But yesterday, Aunt Leona sang about pretty little horsies, and when I asked her if you liked to sing, she said she bet you had a sessy voice."

Rory's eyes bugged out of her head, and she covered the accidental grin with the back of her hand and tried not to snort-giggle. Cody talked for a minute longer while Rory kissed Aaron's forehead and flipped off the light. And when her boy grew quiet and his eyes heavy, she tiptoed back over to the bottom bunk and pressed her ear near the phone.

Cody was singing "Enter Sandman" by Metallica in a soft, deep voice. Oh, dear lord, that wasn't at all appropriate as a lullaby, but it was putting Aaron right to sleep. And as she listened with her head resting against the pillow near her son's, it struck her that the song choice seemed so...Cody. He was new to this dad thing, but it was sexy as hell that he didn't balk against singing a lullaby to his boy. He was a rough and tumble firefighter, up at the station, and probably in a room right next to the other men and women who worked there, but he was totally cool with singing into the phone.

"Aaron?" Cody asked in a voice as soft as a breeze.

"He's asleep," Rory whispered, plucking the phone from Aaron's little hand.

"Ooh," Cody groaned. "Did you hear that?"

She kissed Aaron on the tip of his tiny nose and padded out of the room. "Aunt Leona was right. You do have a sessy voice."

"Shut it," he said, a smile in his tone. "I thought I was singing to a five-year-old audience. Don't tell anyone I did that, or I'll deny it forever."

"Aw, you're just a mushy teddy bear in a gym rat's body."

Cody laughed a deep, booming sound, and she imagined him staring at the ceiling of his tiny station room. She stepped onto the front porch and sank into a rocking chair.

"Do you want to pick us up tomorrow morning, or do you want us to meet you at the restaurant?"

"If you're okay dealing with the big family meeting, I owe you a ride. Is seven too early? I can tell them to meet later if you want."

"No, that's fine." She swallowed hard as she stared at the stars dotting the clear night sky. "I'm nervous."

"Why?"

"I don't want to screw this up. What you said about us being a family earlier—that sounded nice. I mean, I know it's not a real family, because we aren't together like that, but I like that we are going to try to be friends, for Aaron. It's a relief to not feel so alone in all of this. Ugh, sorry. I let this get too heavy."

"I don't mind heavy, Rory. I like when you're honest. And I'm glad you came here and told me about him. It must've been really hard raising him on your own, especially if his little bear is out of control."

"Do you think you can help him?"

"I know I can. Everything is going to be fine. I promise."

Cody sounded so sure of his oath a huge weight

lifted from her chest. Finally, she could breathe easy and not fear the future. If what he said was true, Aaron could be okay. He could lead a normal life, like Cody seemed to be doing.

"I'll see you in the morning, Rory," he said in that low voice of his.

"Okay. G'night, Cody."

When she hung up the phone, she touched her lips as if she'd just been kissed. He'd sung her son to sleep and made her feel safe for the first time in a long time.

But they were just friends, and nothing more. That was how this arrangement worked.

Just friends, right, but that wasn't going to stop her from harboring a top secret crush on Cody-The-Sexy-Fireman-Keller.

SIX

Rory pulled her auburn locks behind her shoulders and considered covering the freckles across her nose with foundation. She'd already done her green eyes up with eye shadow and mascara and plumped her lips with pink gloss, but ever since Aaron had sprouted freckles like hers across his cheeks, she'd started forgoing make-up to cover her own. It seemed the only thing he'd inherited from her.

She pulled her jeans on under her green blouse and hoped this was appropriate attire for meeting Cody's family. No, for meeting Aaron's family. She had to make a good impression for both of the men in her life.

With a deep, steadying sigh, she smoothed the wrinkles from the tight denim material that stretched over her thighs, then pulled on a pair of strappy sandals. She'd even painted her toenails fire engine red this morning.

"He's here!" Aaron called from the front of the house where he'd been perched on the couch in front of the picture window for the past half hour, staring out and waiting for Cody. Aunt Leona was up with the sunrise at a meeting of the Blue-Haired Ladies, so her little man had taken it upon himself to stand watch.

A tiny squeal squeaked past her lips as she tried to expel the nerves. Rushing, she grabbed Aaron's little backpack and a bottled strawberry shake, then opened the door for her bouncing son.

His little legs moved double-time as he pounded the pavement toward Cody. The look of surprise on Cody's face came and went as he reached down and plucked the little boy off the ground. Settling him on his hip, Cody grinned and greeted Aaron. Oh dayum, Cody looked good—backward hat wearing, gray fire department T-shirt clad, wide-shouldered, taper-waisted, muscle-bound, sexy behemoth. She could see the outline of his pecs behind the thin material of his shirt. And when her ovaries were done exploding like Fourth of July fireworks, she guffawed at the jacked up black monster truck behind him with the blackout rims and side rails. Of course, he drove a giant ride. His long, powerful legs wouldn't even fold enough to fit him in her hatchback. And now she was staring at his bicep as it flexed around the back of Aaron's legs, exposing a tendril of tattoo ink along the sleeve of his shirt.

Friends, friends, friends.

"Hey," he greeted her, approaching with long strides. His eyes looked exhausted, but his smile was warm and genuine, and there were those dimples that matched Aaron's. Leaning down, he kissed her on the cheek in the sexiest hello she'd ever been a part of. She wanted to latch onto his leg like a barnacle but held her ground and received the cheek peck with dignity. Or she thought she did until one of her knees locked and she stumbled backward.

His strong hand wrapped around her arm, encircling it completely, and he pulled her upright before she put her tailbone through her throat on the front porch. Bless that man and his many muscles.

"You okay?" he asked, his brows drawing down

in concern.

"Fantastic. I'm fine. Great. But maybe you shouldn't kiss me anymore. On the cheek, I mean. It makes my legs not work. Shit." She covered her mouth and squeaked. "I mean ship. I said ship."

His look of worry had morphed to amusement as Cody witnessed her fast descent into mortification.

"Mommy says ship a lot," Aaron explained. "It's her favorite word."

"Yes, thank you," she whispered in horror. "This is going way better than I imagined."

Cody was laughing now as he hooked his arm around her neck. "You don't have to be nervous. They'll love you."

He smelled divine. Not too strong, like cologne, but a subtle, crisp scent. Maybe his deodorant?

"Are you smelling my armpit?"

"No," she scoffed. "Absolutely not."

"I can hear a lie," he said, his grin growing by the second. "All bear shifters can."

Oh, great. "I'm probably not, but if I was sniffing you, I'd say you smell nice."

The oaf's chest was shaking now with laughter as he led her toward the truck, still holding Aaron.

"You're funny."

No, she was horrified. She hadn't gone to pieces over a man like this since...well, ever. She felt like a teenager mooning over her first crush. Which was stupid, because she was twenty-five years of poise and maturity. Not this bumbling, pit-sniffing motor-mouth.

"What's that?" Cody asked, nodding toward the shake in her hand.

"A protein shake for Aaron. He has to drink them twice a day, per doctor's request."

"A protein shake?" he asked Aaron, who nodded with wide, somber eyes.

"I have to grow big and strong."

"You are big and strong, baby," Rory said. "The doctor just wants to get some weight on you. He's in the bottom percentile for his age."

"That's normal," Cody said.

"It is?"

"Yeah. By the time he hits age seven, you'll be laughing at the fact that you used to give him protein. He and his bear will hit the first big growth spurt around then."

"Cody," Aaron whispered. "Mommy says we

aren't supposed to talk about bears."

Cody frowned and let his arm slip from Rory's shoulders. He came to a stop beside the truck. "Well, that's your mom's call, but around me, you can talk about them, you know why?"

"Why?" Aaron asked as quiet as a breath.

Cody's lips turned up in a heart-stopping smile, and he lowered his voice to match his boy's. "Because I have a bear in me, too. A big one."

Aaron sat ramrod straight in the cradle of Cody's arm, blue eyes bigger than Rory had ever seen them. "Really? Can I see him?"

"Soon. Your mom is right, though. You shouldn't talk about your bear, not without me or her around, okay?"

"I won't."

"Good man." Cody opened the back door of his truck and hefted Aaron into a car seat.

"When did you get that?" Rory asked.

"Uhh, I help do car seat safety courses up at the community center, and I went out on my lunch break yesterday and got one of the seats I recommend in the class." He buckled Aaron in like he'd done it a hundred times, and Rory melted a little more. The man was demolishing the walls she'd erected around her heart.

"Is that part of the fireman gig?"

"You're a fireman?" Aaron asked.

"I am, and someday I'm going to give you a tour of my station."

Aaron clapped his little hands together and yelled excitedly as Cody shut the door. "And yeah, it's part of the gig. We go to schools and teach about fire safety and let the kids climb up on the engine. We get to do a lot in the community. It's part of what attracted me to the job." He led her around the back of the truck and opened her door, then helped her up.

When he was settled behind the wheel, she asked, "What is the other part that attracted you to it?"

"My family. I come from a long line of firefighters. We, meaning shifters, tend to clump together in close-knit groups and pick an occupation. Some of us work in construction or oil rigs. It's usually something physically demanding because the animal side to us requires that to feel steady. I even know a crew of lumberjack bears up in Wyoming. My family, though, we are fire bears. Have been for generations. My brothers work at the same station as me."

"Brothers, plural? How many of you are there?" She was getting nervous all over again at meeting his family.

"Three brothers. Gage is the oldest, I'm next, then Boone and Dade. Gage is mated to a shifter named Leah, and they have two cubs right around Aaron's age. Twins, a boy and a girl, Tate and Arie."

"Do they have bears, too?" Aaron asked from the back seat.

"They sure do, but remember the rule?"

"Don't talk about bears without you or Mommy."

"Good." Cody nodded in approval and smiled into the rearview as he pulled away from Aunt Leona's house.

The truck rumbled loudly as they coasted down Harris Street.

"What are your parents' names?" Rory asked. Perhaps she should be writing this all down so she could remember everyone.

"Ma will just want you to call her Ma. It's her thing. Dad passed when I was young."

"Oh. I'm so sorry." She pulled her gaze straight

ahead and fidgeted with the hem of her shirt. "My dad did too, when I was little, so I know how that is."

Cody glanced at her, his eyes sparking with surprise. "I'm sorry too then."

Rory shrugged away her discomfort with the subject and wiped condensation off the bottled shake. "You don't think he needs these?"

"Nah, he'll grow just fine. We're slow starters is all. If it makes you feel better to give them to him, though, do it. Protein won't hurt him or his animal."

"I don't like the way they taste. It's yucky," Aaron piped up from the back.

"It's so weird talking about his bear so openly. It'll take some getting used to. I've always been paranoid of someone finding out, so we just don't talk about it except around his Changes. He has lots of questions, and most of them I don't have the answers to."

Cody reached over and squeezed her hand, then released it and gripped the steering wheel. "You did good, Rory. You went five years raising a grizzly shifter and didn't get caught. That's a feat in itself. I have the answers for him, but it'll be up to you when you're ready for him to start learning about what he is."

"What do you mean?"

"I mean, that alone time you ruled out? I need that to teach him to control his Changes. If you're around, it'll distract him, and his bear will be a little hellion. Part of growing up a shifter is teaching the animal part of him manners."

"Like disciplining him?" she asked. That didn't sound right. He was just a kid who didn't have his mind when he turned into a bear cub.

"Yeah, but not in the human sense. It's not spankings or time-out, Rory. It's posturing and dominance and growling and figuring out where he belongs in the pecking order. It's him seeing adult grizzlies behaving themselves and learning what he is and isn't supposed to do out in the woods and around humans."

"Oh." Her voice came out small and fragile. "And he can't learn this with me around?" She didn't mean to sound hurt, but she felt left out of a big part of Aaron's life now. If she was like him, a bear shifter, she could help teach him manners. But because she was human, she was supposed to just trust her baby around full-grown grizzlies?

Cody glanced over at her, deep sympathy in the depths of his gaze. "Not on this one. If he's already clawing you when he shifts, he'll need work. You will need to come into this eventually, but not right in the beginning. Hey," he murmured, grabbing her hand again. "If it's too soon, it's too soon. I'm not pushing you, or Aaron. If you need more time to get comfortable with all of this, we'll keep doing it your way."

Her way involved a cage and heartbreak. "No, I think I've accepted my way doesn't work. That's why I'm here. Can we wait a few days, though, until I'm more comfortable with everything?"

"Of course. Whatever you need."

His hand was warm against hers, and boldly she turned her palm over and intertwined her fingers with his. He shot her a surprised glance but didn't pull away. If friends weren't supposed to hold hands, she didn't care right now. Cody's touch felt too good to let go just yet.

Her breath shook as she exhaled her nerves slowly and stared out the window at the passing houses. Aaron had never had an extended family before this, and she was walking into a crew of bear shifters and hoping they would accept her for Aaron's sake.

As Cody parked the truck in the lot behind the donut shop, Rory pulled down the mirror and fretted over her hair, which had decided to curl up like a fiery lion's mane.

"You look beautiful," Cody said, watching her with an unreadable expression.

"What?" she asked softly, sure she'd heard him wrong.

"You look just like I remember." Cody dropped his gaze to the steering column and apologized. "Sorry. That's out of line."

"The friend zone is weird," she said, scrunching up her nose.

"So weird. We kind of did everything backward, didn't we?"

Rory laughed and nodded. "We really did. You look like I remember, too," she admitted quietly. "Better even."

"Flatterer. Come on before you bloat my ego and I can't fit my head through the door."

"Fine. Your muscles are puny, and your towering height and tattoos are wholly unattractive."

"Better," he said with a grin. "Wait there, and I'll get your door."

Inside, a short hallway led to a restaurant that was much smaller than she expected. Or maybe that was because half of the eatery seemed to be taken up by giants. A woman with long, straight, silver hair pulled back in a low ponytail approached first. Her blue eyes, so like Cody and Aaron's, were twinkling with ready moisture.

The woman wrapped Rory up in a hug and whispered, "I always hoped you'd come back."

Rory eased away, baffled. She was a stranger and had done practically nothing to earn this warm affection. "What do you mean?"

Cody squeezed her shoulder and picked Aaron up, then began introducing him to the rest of the people who waited at the bottleneck in the hallway.

The woman lifted a strand of Rory's curled, ruddy hair and studied her with an emotional smile. "You saved Cody from his bond with Sarah. Really, you spared all of us. It's a rare thing to break a bond, and you did it in one night with my son. Do you know he looked for you?"

Rory's heart felt too big for her chest, and her

throat was closing by the second. Her own mother had never been so open and candid, had never strung so many nice thoughts about her in a row like this. "He mentioned he looked for me."

"He searched hard, dear. He was desperate to thank you somehow. We're all so happy you've decided to come back."

Rory's heart dropped to the floor. She hadn't come back from the good of her heart. She'd come back desperate to help Aaron, not for Cody's benefit at all. "I should've come sooner. I'm sorry, Mrs. Keller."

"Oh, honey," Mrs. Keller said, shaking her head and wiping her eyes with the backs of her hands. "You had your reasons for staying away. You were trying to protect your cub. I have four boys of my own and imagine I would've done the same thing if I was afraid their father would put them at risk." She glanced over her shoulder and smiled at Aaron, who was giving a tall man with shoulder length hair and tattoos up his arms a high five. "You raised a strong little cub and kept him safe without the protection of a crew. You're a right proper momma bear. And no more of this Mrs. Keller crap. Call me Ma."

Unable to hold back the tears at Mrs. Keller's offered and undeserved forgiveness, Rory hugged her tight again as another weight lifted off her shoulders. At this rate, she was going to feel free as a bird by week's end.

"Now let me get my arms around my grandson," Ma said, reaching for him.

Aaron gave Rory an uncertain look, but she nodded in encouragement. "This is your grandma."

He reached for her slowly.

Ma plucked him from Cody's grip and swayed gently as she said, "Do you know, you look just like your daddy did at your age?"

"I do?" Aaron asked in that little squeaky voice of his.

"Exactly like," she said, lifting her shoulders so he settled better on her hip.

"Cody, did you hear?" Aaron called over the murmur of the crowd.

"I did, boy, and it's true. I'll show you pictures when we visit grandma's house. You," he murmured to Rory. "You come here. I have some people I want you to meet."

Rory beamed and stepped around Ma.

Nervously, she waved to the three men gathered around Cody.

"Rory, this is Gage." He gestured to a man with dark eyes and darker blond hair that brushed his ears. He nodded a greeting and offered her a friendly smile.

"Boone." Cody clapped the man with the longer blond hair and sleeves of tattoos down his arms. "And this is the baby of the family, Dade." That baby of the family was the tallest one of them all, towering even over Cody.

Rory arched her neck back and whispered, "Holy mayo," as she shook his hand.

Dade laughed and surprised her by pulling her into a rough hug. Boone followed suit, and when she was thoroughly embraced and her spine nice and cracked, Gage pointed to a woman sitting at a table holding a sleeping girl around Aaron's age. The woman had dark hair and eyes and a pixie-like turned-up nose over full, smiling lips. Her eyes danced as she waved.

"This is my mate…I mean wife, Leah. My daughter, Arie. My boy, Tate, is over there trying desperately to get grandma to let your boy down so he can play with him."

Indeed, there was a little dishwater-blond boy jumping up and down, holding onto Ma's shirt with one hand and pleading to play. Aaron was grinning down at him, and they were holding hands.

"Sit by me," Leah offered, patting the long bench seat beside her.

"Okay," Rory said shyly, then scooted all the way through to where Leah sat against the wall. "She's beautiful." She settled beside the woman.

Leah stared down at the girl, blond pigtails piled high and a sleepy smile on her face. "Don't let her fool you. She's a little monster in the mornings. It was easier to just let her fall back to sleep in here."

Rory giggled and said, "Aaron is a morning person."

"Like his daddy."

"Yeah, I'm coming to realize he's a lot like Cody."

Leah looked lovingly at her brother-in-law and then to Aaron. "It looks like the Keller curse has struck you, too."

"What do you mean?" Rory asked.

Leah lifted a lock of her hair, almost as dark as a raven's feather, and set it beside Arie's fair tresses.

"The genetics are strong with those Keller boys."

"Yeah, annoying right?" she joked. "Aaron got freckles. That's my only claim. I carried him for nine months, sick as a dog the entire time, and he came out looking nothing like me and every bit like a little baby Viking."

Leah snorted a laugh and nodded. "Finally, someone who gets my pain."

"Hey, I'm going to order food," Cody said, leaning on the table until his annoyingly sexy triceps flexed. "What do you want?"

"Uhh…" She squinted at the chalkboard menu at the front but it was too blurry to read from this far. "Just get me whatever you're having. I'm not picky. Oh, Aaron will want—"

"A chocolate-covered donut? He's put in his order six times already." Cody winked and sauntered off toward the line with his brothers.

Now, some men looked weird when they winked, but not Cody Keller. Instead, he looked even sexier, oozing all that confidence. It was almost unfair.

"Uh oh," Leah muttered as Ma settled in with Aaron and Tate across the table. "Incoming."

Up at the line, the woman Cody had been with at

the pizzeria approached and pulled him off to the side. Boone snuck a glance behind him, probably to check if Rory was seeing this, and she definitely was.

Ma smiled sympathetically as Rory forced herself to look away. "Shayna is partly our fault. We were encouraging him to date, and she has been relentless for a couple of years now. If it makes you feel any better, I think he was just going out with her to appease me."

"It's none of my business who he sees," Rory said low. "We're just friends."

"Lies," Leah said lightly. "We can hear them."

Rory puffed air from her cheeks and rested her chin on her forearms before she tried again. "It's none of my business who he sees because he said we should only be friends, and he wants us to date other people."

"Truth," Leah said darkly. "That sucks. Why?"

"Because she scares him, that's why," Ma said. "And honey, wielding the ability to scare Cody isn't a bad thing. Give him time."

Time she didn't have. In four days, Rory would be going back to her life. She just hoped the friendship they forged this week would be enough to carry their little team through until the next time she could visit.

Rory glanced up just in time to see the woman kiss Cody on the cheek and slide a narrow-eyed glance her way. Something green and ugly slithered through Rory's veins as she watched the woman walk out the front door.

When she looked back at Leah, the woman was grinning from ear to ear. "You look pissed."

Lifting her chin, Rory said, "I'm unaffected."

"Mm-hmm, I told myself that about Gage for an entire year, and now look at me. Raising his little mini-mes and utterly smitten."

"It's different for Cody and me. We don't really know each other, and if we don't find a way to get along, it'll be Aaron who suffers for it. Cody was right. The safest way to do that is to be friends and focus on our son."

Cody walked back with Boone, but a man stopped him and shook his hand. "Thank you for your service," the man said.

Cody nodded and smiled, then made his way back to the table and slid in beside her, folding his long legs under the table.

"What was that about?" she asked.

Cody shook his head, apparently uncomfortable, but Ma spoke up. "Cody served our country. Two tours."

Rory stared at him. "What? You're military?"

"Was, and I hate talking about it, so let's don't." His voice was hard and cold, snapping like a rubber band, but whether that leftover chill was from his encounter with Shayna or from a haunting experience overseas, she couldn't tell.

"Okay," she murmured as embarrassing heat crept into her cheeks.

From the edge of her vision, she could see him watching her with an unsettled expression, but she didn't care. If he didn't want to talk, and if he wanted to lock her out of that part of his life, fine. They were just friendly strangers anyhow, and it was obviously none of her business.

His hand slid over the top of her thigh, and she tensed, then scrambled over his lap. "I'm going to the bathroom," she muttered as she stumbled off the end of the bench seat.

He didn't get to touch her how he liked after talking to her like that in front of his family. Shocked, she'd asked an honest question. It wasn't like she'd asked him anything too personal. For chrissakes, a stranger shook his hand and thanked him for his service, yet the mother of his child wasn't allowed in on the secret? She felt like grit.

She slipped into the bathroom and locked the door behind her. She didn't really have to pee, but for lack of anything else to do, she gave it the ol' college try, then washed her hands. She could do this. Just friends. She wasn't allowed to ask him about his life until he was ready to bestow his history upon her. Really, that was fair, because she hadn't talked about her parents with him when he'd asked, and he hadn't pushed her to share. She hadn't rejected his question in front of her family, though. Gah, her head was beginning to ache. Puffing air from her cheeks, she turned and unlocked the door.

Cody's giant torso filled the frame, and she squeaked, startled. Without a word, he pushed his way into the bathroom and locked the door behind him.

"What are you doing?" she raged in a whisper. "This is the women's bathroom. No *dicks* allowed."

He crossed his arms over his chest until his arm

muscles bulged. "You're mad."

"I'm not."

Cody shot her a look that called her out on her bullshit and stepped closer. Rory's back bumped the sink as she tried to maintain space between them.

"I'm sorry I snapped at you," he whispered, placing his arms on either side of her, trapping her. "I'm proud of serving, but it wasn't my choice to go to war."

"What do you mean it wasn't your choice? There is no draft."

"There is for my crew. The government knows about us, Rory. We have to do what they want. At the time they asked me to serve, my instincts were screaming to stay with my people. They recruited my brothers, too. They separated all of us while it was my responsibility to protect them."

"Why is everything your responsibility?"

"Because I'm alpha. I'm the leader of the Breck Crew. When my dad died..." Cody swallowed hard and straightened his spine, releasing her from his blue-flame gaze. "When he died, the title went to me."

Rory inhaled deeply. "So people do know about bear shifters."

Cody nodded. "For now it's just the people who want to use their knowledge of our existence as leverage."

"That sucks," she muttered, stunned.

He ran a hand over his short hair and laughed. "You have no idea."

"You know what else sucks?" she asked, crossing her arms.

"What?"

"Shayna."

His golden brows arched high as a slow smile took his face. "You jealous?"

"I mean, it's hard watching someone else kiss the father of your child. I don't care how unattached or mature you are, it's an awkward situation. Even if we're just friends."

A soft knock sounded against the door. "I have to pee." It sounded like Leah.

Cody shot the door a troubled look, and then leveled Rory again with that intense gaze of his. "This is harder than I thought it would be."

"Don't worry, Keller. I'll be out of your hair in four days. Then you can go back to banging whoever you want."

She stepped around him and reached for the doorknob, but he grabbed her arm and spun her to face him. "Don't do that."

"Do what?"

"Call me by my last name and talk about leaving."

His lips crashed down on hers. Inhaling in shock, she balked against him, but he cupped her neck and dragged her waist closer. And as his lips softened and moved against hers, she closed her eyes and melted against him. He angled his head as she ran her hand up his chest. Opening her lips, she allowed him to taste her. A mortifying, helpless sound wrenched from her throat as his fingers turned gentle and the pace of his kiss slowed. He plucked at her lips once. Twice. Resting his forehead against hers, he said, "I shouldn't have done that."

"Don't," she drawled out. "Don't take away from this. What you meant to say is, 'I shouldn't have given you our first kiss in the ladies bathroom of a donut diner.'"

A tiny huff of laughter sounded as he swayed them gently from side to side. "Technically I gave you our first kiss in a bar."

"Yeah, that's not any better, Keller."

"Stop calling me that."

"Don't gripe at me in front of your family."

"Our family now, Dodson."

She narrowed her eyes, readying for a retort when he leaned forward and gave her the sweetest, softest kiss. The kind that ended with a quiet, sexy smacking sound and made her go warm from her mouth to her knees.

"I knew you were trouble from the first time I saw you in that bar, woman."

Leah sang through the door, "I still have to pee."

Cody grabbed Rory's hand and led her out of the bathroom. All she could manage was a drunken smile for Leah.

"What happened to you?" Leah asked, wide-eyed.

She'd been kissed too thoroughly, that's what. Cody looked back at Rory with a wicked grin, then waited for her to climb across the bench seat.

"Where's Aaron?" she asked, panicking when she looked around and he wasn't there.

Ma pointed under the table, and Rory ducked under. Aaron, Arie, and Tate were all playing near her feet with chocolate smiles that said they'd already inhaled their breakfasts.

She huffed a sigh of relief and apologized for bolting.

"No worries," Ma said with a smile as she poured syrup over a pancake so big its edges flopped over the side of the plate. "He's been playing with his cousins and has been perfectly well-behaved. Besides, I'd never let anything happen to him."

"It's true," Boone said. "Ma is scary protective of her grandbabies. She barely lets us hold them."

"Oh, shut up," Ma said with a grin that said she liked being teased.

"Here you go. This is the last of it." A man wearing a T-shirt with a cartoon donut printed on it set two plates stacked high with pancakes, bacon, and eggs over easy in front of her and Cody.

"Oh man, this is too much," she murmured.

"You said to get what I'm having," Cody said with a shrug.

"I didn't realize you required the food of six people."

"I'll finish what you don't eat."

Rory stared at the twin stacks of overflowing food. "Seriously?"

"Just wait until Aaron hits his first growth spurt,"

Gage said from across the table, his plate stacked as high as Cody's. "He'll eat you out of house and home."

She glanced at the half eaten donut that still sat on Aaron's plate and shook her head. Getting him to eat had always been a challenge. "I'll believe that when I see it."

SEVEN

"Are you sure you're up for this?" Rory asked.

Stomachs full of breakfast, they were in line at the train depot, waiting to take a long track around the countryside. The old-fashioned engine behind them hissed steam around their ankles, and Aaron clapped and cheered with the other waiting passengers. He was sitting on Cody's shoulders, high above everyone else, sporting a beaming grin.

Cody, on the other hand, looked utterly exhausted. "I have four more days with you guys, and I don't want to miss anything."

He pulled her against his side with one arm, holding Aaron's legs steady with the other. He leaned closer and murmured, "We had a lot of calls come in last night, and I didn't get any sleep. Usually after the two-day shifts, I go home and sleep the first day away, but I'd rather be with you right now."

Rory wrapped her arms around his waist and rested her cheek against his sternum. "You're a good man, Cody. And a strong one. You aren't invincible, though." She looked up at his tired eyes and the two-day blond stubble on his jaw. "I could go for a nap after this, and Aaron will sleep like a log after the morning he's had."

"Woman, are you seducing me into a family nap with you."

"I am. Is it working?"

The smile dipped from his face, and tenderness filled his eyes as he looked down at her. "I like that you worry about me."

"I like that you forgive easily."

He frowned. "What do I have to forgive you for?"

"For waiting five years to come back."

He rolled his eyes and pulled her toward the loading platform with the other passengers in line. "Ma gave me an earful when I tried to complain to her. Said you were just the right kind of woman for being that protective of your cub." His eyes widened, he looked around, and then lowered his voice. "I mean child. I thought on it, and she's right. You struggled being a single parent for his safety. You're a good mother to my boy. What matters is you came back."

"You aren't mad you missed his firsts?"

"Not mad, Rory. Sad. There's no use cryin' over spilt milk, though. It's done. I can punish you and me both for what happened, or I can try to enjoy the time we have together. And that's what I aim to do." He pressed his lips against her temple, then pulled the train tickets from his back pocket and handed them to the conductor.

Inside, they picked a bench seat in the last car. Cody's hands never left Aaron's back as the boy jumped up and down on the seat by the window. Rory could tell he liked his son by the way he looked at him with a soft smile between amused laughs. He didn't act forced around him or uncomfortable. It was as if he'd been a part of them all along. And it was clear Aaron adored Cody, too. Already, he'd said he wanted to be a firefighter when he grew up.

She was digging through her purse, looking for a package of trail mix she'd put in there in case Aaron got hungry, when an older woman with kind eyes patted her hand. "You sure have a good lookin' family there," she said.

"Thank you," Rory said, feeling breathless.

She stopped her snack search to watch Cody point to someone working on an adjacent track and explain what he was doing to Aaron, who was waving frantically. Life felt so normal here. And sure, part of that was the atmosphere. It was because she was finally back in the place she'd adored so much growing up. And some of that was from Cody's family going out of their way to make her feel so comfortable. But most of it—almost all of it—was from being here with Cody, feeling like a team. Like she wasn't so alone in every single decision about Aaron's future anymore.

What Cody was giving her was more precious than he'd ever know.

****

Rory was so damned beautiful in this light, it was hard to look away from her. He had to, though, or he'd wreck his truck, and today he was carrying precious cargo.

Every minute with her was perfect. She had

opened up something inside of him he'd been scared of, and Rory didn't even have a clue she was doing it. This was effortless for her, settling his bear and making the animal inside of him feel manageable for the first time in as long as he could remember.

Lodgepole pines and towering spruces blurred by, creating a green canvas behind her dark red hair and making her smiling eyes look even brighter when she looked at him. He'd only felt this strongly for one other woman, and Sarah hadn't deserved his devotion. Rory was different, though. She was good and honest. Hardworking and a good mother. She was funny as hell, even when she wasn't trying to be, and sometimes when she looked up at him, her beauty stunned him. Even exhausted, the hum of excitement in his blood had been constant today.

Six years ago, he'd told himself he'd searched for her to thank her, but that was bullshit. He'd searched for her because he'd been desperate for moments like this.

The road forked, and he explained, "We're in Blue River now. Ma lives up that road, and that middle one leads to my brothers' cabins. This one goes to mine." He took the left vein and turned onto a switchback.

"Aw, it's like a werebear commune."

"Bear shifter commune," he corrected as he pulled in front of his cabin.

"Oh wow," Rory said, staring out the window. "It's beautiful."

Okay, he hadn't gone for *beautiful* when he'd drawn up the plans and hired a contractor to help him build it. He'd gone for man-cave chic, but he could see the appeal for Rory. Set against a snow-peaked mountain backdrop and out in the middle of nowhere, this place was a safe haven for shifters like him and Aaron.

The cabin had been constructed of logs, and the roof was steep and dove all the way to the ground to ward off massive amounts of snow in the wintertime. He pulled Aaron from his car seat and grabbed the little blue backpack he took with him everywhere he went, then led Rory down the flagstone sidewalk.

For the first time today, nerves kicked in, and he struggled to get the key in the lock. It mattered if she liked his den or not. She was the first person, outside of family, he'd ever invited up here.

Aaron looked around with a sleepy, slow blink as

Cody hugged him tighter to his hip and led Rory through the living room. There were only two bedrooms and a kitchen for the main touring rooms, so not five minutes later, he was standing back in the middle of the master bedroom, holding Rory's hand and imagining her all tangled up in his sheets.

He settled Aaron down against the thick green comforter, and the little boy curled his legs to his chest immediately. Rory pulled a brown fuzzy blanket from the backpack and placed it in Aaron's arms.

"Cody, meet Bebe—Aaron's comfort item since birth."

Canting his head and resting his hands on his hips, he watched Rory slip under the covers with their son. Her auburn hair fanned over the pillowcase as she tucked Aaron up against her and made room for Cody to take the other side.

How had he gotten this lucky?

"You look mushy," she said with a smile in her voice.

Cody rearranged his face as hard as he could and deepened his frown. "Better?"

"Yes. You look much tougher now."

He kicked off his shoes and hit the switch for the

ceiling fan, then closed the curtains until the room was dark. A trilling noise came from his pocket, and he shimmied his phone out and looked at the screen.

Unknown, the caller ID read. Shit.

He cast Rory an apologetic glance, then let himself out of the room and shut the door gently behind him.

"Hello?" He bit the word out, already aware of who was on the other end.

"Keller, we need to talk."

"Why?"

"Can you meet me in an hour?"

"No, Krueger. I'm busy, and I have nothing more to say to you."

"I need you for another mission."

With a sigh, he made sure the bedroom door was still closed, then padded across the room to the other bedroom and lowered his voice. "You don't think I've done enough? The answer is no."

A beat of silence led to a huffed and cruel-sounding laugh. "Fuck being nice about it then. Keller, you'll do the mission. I'm not asking you. I'm telling you. We have a target, and we know where he'll be tomorrow night."

"I'm not your fucking assassin, Krueger. I'm a firefighter."

"No, you're a weapon. A weapon we've created, and one we'll destroy if you push our hand. All of the fight training and your time in the field have made you invaluable to me. And your unique abilities and heightened senses, your instincts…well, those are what have made you the perfect assassin."

"I'm not going to kill for you anymore. I served my time. You said you'd out us and make us register publicly as shifters if I fought my orders, and this is me calling your bluff. Out us, and you'll have no weapons left."

"I'd never out you, Keller. But if we have a superior race, a genetically enhanced one, that has suddenly gone rogue and out of control, we won't hesitate to annihilate your entire species to keep the American public safe."

Cody's heart hammered against his sternum. "What the fuck does that mean?"

"It means you'll do this mission and every other one we need you for, or I won't stop until every crew of bear shifters has been eradicated. Don't test me, Keller. The continuation of your species depends on your pliability."

Cody stared at the wall, chest heaving as his bear clawed him from the inside to escape.

"Oh, and Keller? I know about Rory Dodson and your cub."

The line went dead, and Cody barely stifled the urge to throw his phone against the wall just for the satisfaction of watching it splinter into a hundred fractured pieces. He flipped it onto the couch instead and gripped his hair. "Fuck."

"Cody?" Aaron said from right behind him. "I don't feel good."

Cody turned just in time to see the boy's eyes turn gold. His little body jerked inward, and the sound of snapping bones filled the room.

"No!" Cody gasped, then grabbed him around his middle as fur sprouted from Aaron's skin. Dodging furniture, he raced out of the house and settled Aaron's shifting form onto the softest looking patch of grass in the front yard. Pulling frantically at his shirt, Cody undressed and kicked out of his jeans just as Aaron stood fully Changed and swaying on all fours.

The little brown bear cub looked up at him, eyes

round and mouth hanging open. He spun and bolted, and Cody cursed as he gave the bear inside of him permission to have his skin. Pain, blinding and bright, made him lose sight of the cub for a moment, but he was thundering after his scent as soon as the Change was through.

Damn, his cub was fast. The tiny pants and snarls of fear that drifted to him on the wind drove Cody to charge after him faster. It wasn't until he came to a bottleneck between two boulders and a patch of brambles beyond that he caught up to Aaron. The cub was caught in the thorny vines, squalling in pain.

Cody rattled a low, comforting sound from his throat as he pulled the baby bear from the thorns. Aaron struggled against him—not surprising since he'd never been around an adult bear before. Cody hugged him tighter and sat on his haunches as he rocked him gently from side to side. It took a long time, but eventually, Aaron wore himself out fighting, biting, and scratching. And after time, his snarls of terror faded to the baby noises of a cub who was comfortable. He nuzzled against Cody's chest, snuffing as the humming grew louder in the little cub's chest. This was as close to purring as bears got.

With a deep sigh of relief, Cody settled Aaron down and turned away immediately, leaving the choice to his cub whether to follow or not. If he could smile in this form, he would've when he heard the soft footsteps following right along after him.

Cody showed Aaron his forest. Time was nothing out here in the woods where everything had a smell and a sound. Where he could watch his cub explore the rocks and moss. Where he could witness Aaron scenting a deer trail or raking his tiny claws down a sapling just to feel like a powerful wee bear. He would grow brawny and tall someday, but here in his woods, Cody witnessed a first—Aaron's first Change out of a cage and in the wild where he belonged.

As the sun began to set behind the trees, Cody called a short bellow for Aaron to leave the shallow creek rapids he'd been chasing minnows in and follow him home.

Rory waited on the porch steps as they cleared the tree line, and Aaron immediately charged. He wasn't thinking straight in his animal form, and that had to change. Keeping his head while he was a bear would make Aaron's life easier, safer.

Reaching forward, Cody clipped his tiny legs out

from under him with a gentle rake of his giant paw. And when Aaron got up, eyes intent on Rory, Cody pulled him back and slammed his feet on either side of the cub as he let out a deafening roar to break his focus on Rory.

Aaron crouched, ears flattened and eyes startled. Cody looked down at him, blasting breath through his lungs and daring the little beasty to charge again.

Rory was now standing in the yard, still as a stone and pallid as a ghost. Understandable since Cody was twice her height if he stood on his hind legs. He wouldn't ever hurt her, though.

She didn't know it yet, but she was his to protect.

Aaron followed slowly, and as Cody approached, Rory put her hands over her face and whispered, "Please don't hurt me."

Cody pressed his forehead against the warmth of her stomach and rocked her back gently, then ran the side of his face against her ribcage. Tentative fingers touched the fur at the scruff of his neck. Rory sniffled as a drop of wetness patted against his ear.

Cody looked over his shoulder, giving Aaron permission to approach. The scent of Rory's fear thickened the air. She'd been hurt by her cub before.

If Cody hadn't seen the scars on her arm, he would've known it from the acrid smell of her terror now.

Aaron charged a few feet, bluffing, and Cody swatted his behind and let off a low, rumbling warning.

Slowly, Rory knelt down and offered her closed fist for Aaron to sniff. He wove back and forth, nervously shifting his weight from side to side, but at last, he came close enough for Rory to touch his fur.

"My baby bear," she crooned.

The look of recognition that sparked in Aaron's eyes had Cody taking a step back to give them space. Aaron latched his mouth onto her arm, but it wasn't an attack. The humming sound reverberating from the little cub's chest gave away his intentions. He wouldn't bite her hard enough to pierce her skin or Turn her. This was a sign of affection for his caregiver. The whites of Rory's eyes shone all around her mossy green irises, but she didn't balk or run. His brave human. No, she sat down in the dirt and pulled Aaron into her lap as the cub mouthed her arm and hummed.

When she looked back up at Cody, her eyes were filled with tears. His first instinct was to blight out whatever had made her upset, but the grateful smile on her lips settled him.

"You don't even know what you've done for us," she said, voice hitching. "Thank you."

And as he sat back, watching his accidental family cuddling in his front yard, Cody knew he would accept Krueger's mission. He'd do anything, even at the cost of his own soul, if it meant Rory, Aaron, and the rest of the Breck crew were safe.

The weight of being alpha had been great.

The weight of being a father was greater.

EIGHT

"Did you see me, mommy?" Aaron asked in that tiny voice of his. "I wasn't even in a cage, and Cody said I did good."

"Baby, I did, and I'm so proud of you. Was it scary being out in the woods?"

Aaron frowned and shook his head slightly. "I don't remember. Cody's bear is giant," he said, stretching his arms wider than the pillow he was laying on.

He'd scarfed down a grilled cheese sandwich and mixed vegetables but had barely been able to keep his eyes open at the dinner table. Cody said it was normal, and that he needed to get sleep now.

She pulled the burgundy comforter from the foot

of Cody's guest bed up to Aaron's chin and gave him tiny kisses all over his face. He giggled, then stifled a yawn. The poor kid had dark bags under his eyes like he always did after a Change. He looked like he hadn't slept in a week, but at least this time, he seemed happier.

"Cody?" he called softly.

His father appeared in the doorframe and smiled. "What do you need, kiddo?"

"Can you sing me that lullaby?"

"Uh." Cody dropped his gaze and ran his hand over his short hair. If Rory didn't know better, she could've sworn he was blushing. "Sure."

Rory left them to it, kissing Aaron's forehead once more before she left the dark room. Sitting on the couch, she could hear the lyrics of the heavy metal song drift through the house, and she smiled despite the stress of the last few hours.

It was nearly half an hour before Cody emerged. He'd been quiet since his shift with Aaron. She thought he'd come sit on the couch with her, but instead he wouldn't meet her eyes as he strode into the laundry room. Earlier, he'd thrown the clothes from his fire department duffle bag along with

Aaron's jeans into the washer and now seemed busy transferring the damp garments to the dryer.

Standing from the comfortable cushion of the couch, she made her way toward the laundry room. "Did I do something wrong?" she asked as she leaned against the doorway.

"No."

"But you're upset."

"I'm fine." Cody closed the dryer door and turned it on, then leaned back against it and let off an explosive sigh. "Ma wants to throw a big barbecue tomorrow for you and Aaron."

"Where?"

"Here."

"So," she said, kicking the corner of the doorway with the toe of her wedge heel, "*you're* throwing a barbecue."

"Basically."

"But that's not what you're upset about," she guessed.

Cody shook his head, but didn't offer an explanation.

"Is it me?"

Another shake of his head, and he looked as tired

as Aaron had.

"Is this one of those things like the tours you served? You don't want to talk about it with me?"

This time he nodded his head once and left his chin on his chest.

"That's okay," she murmured, sliding her arms around his waist. She rested her cheek against his thrumming heartbeat. "I stormed your life, and you don't owe me explanations. I know it'll take time to trust me."

He ran his fingers through her hair. "This has nothing to do with trusting you. It's about protecting you."

She arched her face back and searched the worry in his eyes. "Do you remember the first time we were together?"

"Do I remember the *only* time we were together? Yes." His brow winged up in a challenge. "Do you?"

"I was completely sober."

He laughed and ran both of his hands through her hair now. "You were drunk as a skunk. I wanted to wait until we were both sober, but you weren't having any of that. Temptress."

"I wanted what I wanted," she mused

unashamedly.

"Regrets?"

"None. You gave me Aaron that night. You?"

He shook his head slowly and searched her face as if he'd never seen anything like her. "None."

Spinning her so fast, her stomach dipped, Cody set her up on the dryer. The metal was warm under her legs, heated from working. The vibrations felt surprisingly erotic as he pulled her knees wider and settled in between her thighs.

"Tell me, Rory," he whispered, pressing his lips against her neck in a nibbling kiss. "Did you ever think of me when you touched yourself?"

Her breath shook as he pulled her to the edge of the dryer and rolled his hips against hers.

"Well?" he murmured as he trailed his mouth up to her sensitive earlobe. "Did you?"

"Yes," she panted out.

"Good." Easing back, he pulled her shirt over her head and snapped his fingers against the clasp of her bra. It fell forward and she shrugged out of it.

Cody kicked the door closed and tugged his T-shirt over his head. The words *Veni, Vidi, Vici* were tattooed in cursive across his rippling chest, and more curls of ink stretched from his collar bone down one arm. His abs flexed with each breath as his gaze ravished her body. God, he made her burn.

His skin was smooth and hard under her fingers as she traced the striations in his shoulders. But when he lifted his eyes again, he looked uncertain. Lost even.

She cupped his cheek and kissed him softly to put his fears at ease. He was afraid she'd leave again, but that was beyond her now. She couldn't go back to Oklahoma and raise Aaron alone—not knowing that Cody was right here waiting for them to come back so he could be a part of their lives.

Jaw working under her palm, Cody thrust his tongue against hers and pulled her close until her breasts pressed against the hard planes of his chest. His skin felt divine next to hers. The kisses between them toed the edge of desperation as Cody unsnapped the button of her jeans.

The rip of her zipper had her arching against him as he nibbled his way down her throat. As he peeled off her pants, he latched onto her nipple, drawn up tight from the pleasure he had built inside of her. His tongue laved against the sensitive skin there, and she pulled his head closer.

"I need..." What did she need? Everything. All of him, but how to ask that of a man who wasn't comfortable sharing himself yet?

A soft growl resonated from his chest as he pulled her lacy panties to the side. She didn't even have time to balk in shock before his mouth was on her sex.

Hoooly mayo. She threw her head back as she ran her fingers through his short hair. The man definitely still remembered where her clit was. He tongued it gently, over and over until she was on the verge of release, then he angled his chin and pressed his tongue deeply inside of her. She was gasping for breath now, watching his head bob between her legs. The growling sound he'd been making earlier was getting louder by the moment, and as the pressure increased to unbearable levels, she whispered, "I'm coming!" a moment before her orgasm seized around his clever tongue. Pulsing aftershocks went on and on as he continued his affection.

"One," he growled out, lifting her off the dryer and carrying her like she weighed less than air into his bedroom.

Her heart raced with the realization that he had more sexy plans for her. His eyes reflected like an animal's in the dim light from the bathroom, but she wasn't afraid. Not after earlier when he'd protected her from her own cub. Cody would never hurt her.

With his foot, he kicked the door closed, then set her gently on his bed. "Let me get a condom," he whispered against her lips, then kissed her. His weight disappeared.

"Wait! Leah said you don't get sick. Not like humans."

"We don't."

"I'm on the pill."

His movements by the nightstand stopped, and he turned slowly.

She sat cross-legged on his bed, mortification heating her cheeks. "I want to feel you."

His eyes sparked with hunger as he crawled over the covers toward her, his arms flexing as he approached. Her breath caught in her throat when she dragged her gaze down his torso to the long erection he'd unsheathed between his legs. This part she'd forgotten about—how big he was. He wasn't just long, but thick, too. Intimidatingly so.

"Don't be scared," he said on a breath. "I'd never hurt you."

She smiled as the dim light illuminated one side of his face and cast the other in shadow. She'd just been thinking that moments ago, how he'd never hurt her. "I know."

Cody nudged her knees apart with his and settled his hips against hers. The head of his cock brushed her wet seam, and she rolled her hips instinctively, chasing him.

"More of that," she whispered, running her hand down his steely arm.

The corner of his mouth turned up slightly as he pushed into her slowly, filling her, stretching her until she had to remind herself to relax or she wouldn't be able to take all of him. Damn, he felt good as his hips bumped hers. Her nerve endings were sensitive right now after his thorough attention in the laundry room.

Cody closed his eyes as he pulled out of her, and when he opened them again, they were the gold-green wild color that said his animal was awake and with her. She loved him like this. Open and vulnerable—allowing her to see all of him, even the secret places he hid from everyone else.

He pressed into her again, bucking his powerful hips as he clenched his jaw. He was trying to be gentle with her, and it made her love him more.

Love.

Could it be that the stranger who'd fathered her child could be the one who belonged to her? She'd never dared to hope before, but here in the dim light, with his eyes on hers as he moved within her, she knew it was true. He was hers.

The realization loosened her chest as tingling pressure built with each brush of his pelvis against her clit. Cody was hers and worth fighting for. His breathing turned to panting as a frown took his face, as if he was feeling the same revelation she was. His eyes widened as he pumped into her faster.

"Tell me to stop now, or I won't be able to," he rasped out in a growly voice she didn't recognize.

Confused, she held onto him tighter. "I don't want you to stop."

"I can't... I can't..." His eyes were growing brighter as he rammed into her, pushing her farther up the bed with each stroke.

Cries of ecstasy escaped her parted lips as he

pulled at the backs of her knees and spread her wider. He slammed into her, bucking faster until she clawed at his back and panted out his name.

As her body clenched with the first pulses of her explosive orgasm, jets of warmth shot into her, heating her from the inside out. Cody gripped her hair and emptied himself completely. Pleasure and pain blinded her for an instant, and she gasped and bowed against him.

"Shit," Cody gritted out, clutching his chest. He pulled out of her, and wetness trickled down her legs. Scrambling backward, he nearly fell off the bed trying to escape her.

"What's wrong?" she asked, staring at his hand as he clutched his chest. Baffled, she looked down at her own chest, where she seemed to be burning.

"Tell me you feel it, Rory. Please, God." His eyes held agony as he shook his head.

She'd never seen a man like him scared before now.

"Please tell me you feel it, too," he pleaded.

"It hurts," she whispered, rubbing the tender place in between her breasts. "What did we just do?"

Cody's chest heaved as he searched her face. "I think I just bonded us."

NINE

Cody sat on the edge of the bed with his back to her. He was fighting a fear she could only imagine. Whatever his bond with Sarah had done before Rory had come along, it had scarred him deeply.

Slowly, she crawled to him and placed her hand on the hardened cords of muscle in his back. It took minutes of her rubbing gently over the entire expanse for him to relax under her touch.

"The scariest day of my life was when I had Aaron," she admitted for the first time out loud. "I was sure I wouldn't be good enough, fit enough, firm enough. I was just afraid I wouldn't be enough. My mom disowned me when she found out I was having a child out of wedlock. She is conservative about things like that. My friends were twenty and in college. They were clubbing and drinking and worrying about final exams while I was growing a baby. I had no one except for Aunt Leona, and she lived states away. I had Aaron alone. No one was in the hospital room holding my hand or telling me everything would be all right, and I was so scared. I don't know what happened between you and Sarah, but I know that look on your face because I've seen it in the mirror many times. If you're scared of me, Cody Keller, I want you to know that you are enough."

"You'll leave," he said low. "And not just in a few days. Someday you'll see everything. All of the terrible things I've done to protect my people. The lines I've crossed. You'll see how dark I am inside, and you'll run and never look back."

"I'm not running anymore. I'll stay. All you have to do is ask."

His gaze jerked to hers. "You'll stay here? You and Aaron? With me?"

"A bond is a big thing, right?"

A nod as he pivoted his shoulders and rubbed her thigh with his warm hand.

"And it would hurt you if I took Aaron and left?"

A wince and another nod.

"Well," she said, heart in her throat. "It would hurt me deeply, too. I can't imagine driving away anymore. I don't want to break up the family we have. And I don't care if it isn't like others. If we aren't married or if we're still calling ourselves 'friends.' Our family can be different because we're different. All I know is Aaron..." She paused as tears burned her eyes and she tried to regain control of herself. "Aaron has never smiled so much. And for me? I've never been happier than when I'm with you. I broke your bond with Sarah because you didn't belong with her. You belong with me."

A hopeful smile, soft and slow, transformed his face. "Are we really doing this?"

"If you'll have us. I mean, I'll have to find a job here and a place to live and—"

Cody's lips collided with hers, and he pulled her over his lap until she straddled his hips. "We'll figure everything out," he promised. "Together."

Easing back, she cupped his cheeks and searched his dancing eyes. "Are you happy?"

"Yes."

"No more fear?"

Darkness slashed across his features for an instant before he composed his face again. “Not about us. Not now.”

“My brave monster not scared of a little human anymore.”

Cody pulled her down to the bed and curled his body around her, pressing his chest against her shoulder blades. “I would’ve been there for you if I’d have known. I would’ve been in that hospital when Aaron was born, telling you everything was going to be all right.”

“I know. I had all these reasons for keeping you out of our lives, but now they all seem silly.”

“When is his birthday?”

“January ninth. He was seven pounds even when he was born and started sleeping through the night at just four weeks.”

“Good baby.”

“He was amazing. I had to drop out of college when he was born, but finished my degree online.”

“Did you walk the stage?”

“No. No one was there to see it, and I didn’t have anyone to take care of Aaron.”

“I’m sorry your mom disowned you. I can’t

imagine feeling angry enough at Aaron to abandon him if he needed me like that."

"Yeah. That was the hardest part of it all. Just…feeling alone. These last few days have been amazing. Even if someone is there helping watch him with me, I feel so much more relaxed."

"Does he play sports yet?"

"Not yet. Preschool was all I could handle."

"Would you mind if I signed him up for T-ball next season? I could coach. It would be good for him to get into sports and learn about teamwork. My brothers and I all play on an intramural baseball team each spring and fall. It helps settle the animal if we stay active."

"I think he would love playing T-ball," she said with a grin at the wall. She stroked his arm that was hooked around her stomach and snuggled back against him. "I'll like watching you play, too."

She imagined nachos and bleachers, suicide sodas and ball caps. And Cody in a pair of tight baseball pants. Yep, she was going to watch the hell out of him playing some intramural sports.

"I'm going to go check on Aaron," Cody murmured. He stood and pulled his jeans on. "It's a new place and a new bed. I'll be right back."

Propping herself up on her elbow, she watched him saunter out of the room. He was going to find out real quick Aaron slept like the dead, but it was incredibly endearing that he was worried. She'd checked on Aaron three times a night for years when he was a baby, paranoid that he'd suddenly stop breathing.

She couldn't imagine what Aaron had done to Cody's already protective instincts.

She'd been so scared to come back here for Aaron's sake, and now, she couldn't imagine their lives without Cody. Hitting rock bottom had ended up being her salvation. Without the desperation for a better future for her son, she would've never seen Cody again.

Without rock bottom, she and the man she was falling in love with would've never had a shot at a second chance.

****

The morning had flown by. Cody had dropped her off at Aunt Leona's at dawn, thanks to some meeting he had to go to in town. She'd made pancakes for Aaron and her aunt and gotten ready for the day. With a couple of hours left before the barbecue, Rory had walked into town with her aunt and son to ride the ski lifts to the top of the mountains. They still ran in the summer for the scenic views. At the very top, where the air was thinner, there were concession stands and rides. The lift was enclosed with carpet seats and windows all around. As soon as the door shut, Aaron had stood against the window and chattered on about all of the animal prints he could see in the creak mud below. And after they'd come back down the mountain, they'd walked down Main Street.

Much to Aunt Leona's giggling delight, Rory picked up job applications at the museum, a tourist T-shirt shop, and a couple of restaurants. If she was serious about setting down roots here, she needed an income and a place to stay. She and Aaron couldn't live in Aunt Leona's bunk beds forever, and she wanted to take things slow and steady with Cody. Moving in together felt like rushing, and this time around, she wanted to give their relationship a real shot.

Rory stopped by a quaint real estate shop in the middle of town and picked up a magazine full of rentals. There wasn't a shortage since tourism ruled Breckenridge. She would fill out the applications tonight and bring them back when she was in town again.

A half hour before the barbecue was to begin, they meandered up the sidewalk toward Harris Street. Aaron was scarfing down a strawberry and chocolate-filled crepe from a roadside vendor. His appetite had been much improved today. Maybe it was because he was happier, but she suspected it had something to do with his long Change and adventure in the woods with Cody yesterday. She was still in awe that he'd been able to manage Aaron. Cody seemed to have a natural instinct when it came to their son.

"My messy little moose," she mused, stooping to wipe his chocolate mustache with a wad of napkins she's swiped from the crepe shop.

Aaron looked up at her with wide, happy eyes and smacked his lips. "This is my new favorite second breakfast."

"Second breakfast?"

"Cody says second breakfast can be yummier than first breakfast."

"Why am I not surprised that man can put away food like that?" Aunt Leona asked. "He's a beefcake. Gotta feed that meat."

Rory snorted, then blushed as she remembered Cody's tatted, muscle-ripped body covering hers last night. "They work out a lot up at the station to stay fit for the job. Have you seen his brothers?"

"Oh, honey, the Blue-Haired Ladies have seen all of those Keller boys. Everyone has. They're pretty to look at, sure, but they are also local heroes. The town celebrated when those boys came back from the war. Both times. And every one of them is involved in the community. Not the political, boring part of it either. They help with all of the fundraisers, fire safety classes, and parades. They even visit the schools around here and let the kids tour the engine. Those Keller boys are good to the bone, every last one of them. You couldn't have picked a better daddy for your baby if you tried."

Rory smiled sadly as she watched Aaron bound ahead and run a stick along a metal fence, half-eaten crepe dripping chocolate from his other hand. "I wish Mom could meet him. Maybe she'd feel better about everything if she saw what a good man he is."

"Well, if she got anywhere close to Cody Keller, I think he'd charm the socks off her. My sister is a stubborn woman, though. She always has been."

"Have you talked to her lately?" Rory asked softly.

"Two weeks ago. She's doing well. She's dating some attorney and is living in the suburbs now."

"It's so strange not knowing about my own mom's life after growing up so close with her."

"Yeah, I imagine it would be. Rory, you know none of what happened between you and your mom is your fault, right?"

Rory plucked a tender lime-green leaf from a bush as she passed and folded it neatly. "I'd argue it's all my fault. I was the one who had the baby against her advice."

"That was on your mother, child. She should've never given an ultimatum like that. And her not wanting to get to know her grandson..." Aunt Leona stared after Aaron with a sad shake of her head. "She's missed out on more than she'll ever know. That was her choice, though, and I have gone blue in the face harping on her for treating you like that. She only talks to me on the phone if I don't bring up the past."

"Or me."

Aunt Leona's thin lips quirked up in a sympathetic smile as she hugged her against her side and patted Rory's shoulder. "I'm glad you are your own woman, Rory Dodson. You didn't let other's opinions bring you down or change your mind. You stuck to your guns and showed impressive poise in how you have raised your son. Your good parenting shows in how happy and well-adjusted Aaron is. You're a good momma."

Emotion congealed in her chest, and Rory looked away before Aunt Leona could see how much those words touched her. She'd longed to hear any compliment from Mom when she was younger, but being a mother to Aaron was different than making straight As or getting a college scholarship. It was the most important thing she'd ever done, and to hear Aunt Leona, whose opinion mattered so much, tell her she was good at this...well, it meant the entire world.

"What's that?" Aaron asked from up ahead. He bolted for the front door of her aunt's house and picked up a vase of daylilies. "Mommy, I think it's for you."

When Rory reached him, she read the scribbled card aloud. "I didn't get to do all this stuff the first time around. I'll make it up to you. Can't wait to see you and Aaron. Bring your swimsuits. Cody"

"Oh, I love daylilies. Sweet, sweet man. Does he have a pool at his house?" Aunt Leona asked.

Rory frowned at the card, rereading it silently. "No. Not even a creak that I saw."

"I wonder why you need swimsuits then."

"Beats me."

TEN

It became clear why they needed swimsuits when Rory pulled her little hatchback up the gravel road toward Cody's cabin. Out front, on the gently sloping lawn, Boone and Dade were unrolling a giant tarp, and Cody was hosing it down and squirting dish soap on it. A tub of water balloons sat off to the side. Beside him, Arie and Tate were bouncing up and down in oversize T-shirts. Rory could practically hear them from here, begging the Keller boys to hurry up and let them slide down.

"Mommy!" Aaron yelled when he saw the festivities out front. "Do you see that?"

"I do, baby."

"What is that?"

“It’s a homemade Slip ’N Slide. You run real fast and lay down on it and slide all the way down to the bottom of the hill.”

“I want to do it!” He rolled down his window and yelled, “Hi Arie! Hi Tate!”

The twins waved and called out squeaky greetings.

Rory couldn’t help her grin if she tried for a hundred years. Aaron had a family and cubs his own age he could grow with. He wouldn’t feel so different here. Now, his future stretched on and on, and the potential for him to lead a happy life had improved tenfold.

She’d been afraid Aaron would have to hide what he was forever, but the Breck Crew offered sanctuary.

Cody’s smile made her knees knock as she parked the car at the end of a row of pickup trucks and jeeps. He handed Arie the hose and jogged over as she opened her door. Offering her a hand up, he dragged his gaze from her green bikini top to her cutoff jean shorts to her flip-flop clad feet.

“Damn, woman,” he murmured.

“Cody!” Aaron hollered. “I’m stuck.”

With a rapid blink as if he was coming out of a

trance, Cody pulled open the back door and freed Aaron from his car seat restraints. The little boy hopped from the car and blasted into Cody's legs, hugging him so hard his little fists clenched the denim material of his jeans. He kissed Cody's knee with a loud smack, then bolted a beeline up the hill for Arie and Tate, his little shark-print swim trunks sagging under his neon blue tank top.

Cody watched him with an expression that would be called soft if it were on a softer man's face. Cody, however, was all chiseled jaw line and intense eyes. On him, it just looked like pride.

Rory stepped under his outstretched arm and nuzzled her cheek against the cotton material of the white T-shirt he was wearing, right against the fire department logo over his heart.

With a crooked grin, he grabbed her ass and squeezed as he leaned down and kissed her lips. He plucked the strap of her bikini and said, "You are a sight for sore eyes."

"Did you miss us?"

"Of course, I did. You're going to make those long shifts up at the station real hard on me, aren't you?"

She walked slowly beside him toward the rest of

the crew gathered in plastic lawn chairs around a fire pit. "What are the rules with that? Are we allowed to visit?"

"Visits are tough because we never know when a call is going to come in. It's almost Fourth of July, so fireworks have been a problem lately. On slow days you can, though."

"What about calling you?"

"Yeah, there is no rule against calling. I'll pick up if I'm able and call you back if I'm busy. And if I can find time, I'll try to call around Aaron's bedtime. Hey, I need to tell you something." He pulled her to a stop and gripped her shoulders. "Shayna is our dispatcher. We don't work in the same building, but I wanted you to find out from me. I have to talk to her still, professionally."

"Oh. That's okay." Did she like the idea of Shayna still having any kind of relationship with Cody, professional or otherwise? No. But he was telling her up front because he obviously didn't want to pursue anything with the woman. "Thanks for telling me." With a put-upon sigh, she said, "I suppose I'll have to stop calling my exes if we're going to date exclusively."

His eyes narrowed. "What exes?"

"Joke."

With a growl, he threw her over his shoulder and strode toward the fire pit as she giggled. "Wait, I brought desert! And towels. And I need to shut my car door!"

He spun so fast it made her stomach lurch back into her kicking toes. He shouldered the bag she'd stuffed with towels and sunscreen, balanced the homemade pink lemonade pie she'd thrown together this morning, then kicked the door closed, all while stabilizing her on his shoulder with a cleverly placed hand on her ass. The sexy brute.

He leaned over and bit her waist gently, then hesitated and stopped. "What is that?"

Settling her on her feet, he jutted his chin at the pair of silver lines delving down her hips. "Did Aaron make those scars, too?"

"Yep," she said, turning so he could see the matching ones on the other side. "Stretch marks, Keller. Your son scarred me up good."

Cody's eyes went round, and he leaned down to study them. Running his fingertip down one, he said, "You got these growing my boy?"

Cody was tough and the strongest man she'd ever met to shoulder what he did. But when he said things like that, words that exposed an inner and unexpected sweetness to a man so rough, it melted her. "Yes," she said on a breath. "Do you think they're unsightly? It's my first time in a swimsuit in front of other people since…you know."

He lifted his eyes to hers, and unmistakable honesty pooled in their blue depths as he said, "They're so fucking beautiful." A wicked grin slid over his lips. "I want to bite them. I'm *going* to bite them."

A delicious shiver trembled up her spine and landed in her shoulders. "Cody," she murmured out a warning, "you can't be saying things like that to me when we're about to go have a coherent conversation with your family."

He slid his arm over her shoulders and dragged her toward the Breck Crew. Pulling her in close, he whispered against her ear, "I like when your eyes get all drunk-looking when I talk to you."

"Yeah, well I like it when you sport public boners, so we're even." She arched her eyebrows at the bulge in his pants.

"I'm not ashamed," he whispered, then patted

her butt and moved off to a table of covered food.

Rory stood there watching him as her body heated from the inside out like a volcano. Cody's jeans encased his powerful stride just right, and the shirt he wore clung to his thick shoulders. His torso tapered into a V-shaped waist. He stood tall and strong as he sauntered away, as if he knew his exact place at the top of the food chain around here—the sexy beast of a man.

"Hey," Ma said, squeezing her neck. "Look here. I stayed up late last night trying to find this for you." She pulled a photo album off an empty chair and handed it to Rory.

Rory took the seat in between Ma and Leah and opened the album to the first crackling page.

"Oh my gosh, Ma!" Leah squealed. She adjusted the strap of her red and white striped one-piece swimsuit and scooted closer. Tucking her dark, wavy tresses behind her ear, Leah giggled at the picture of four little boys in too-short shorts and matching shirts. Each of the brothers held little yellow fishing poles and donned matching gap-toothed grins. The Keller men were a couple years apart in age, but here, besides a little height difference, they could've been multiples.

Rory ran her finger across the wild grass at the bottom of the picture and grinned from ear to ear.

"You know which one's Cody?" Ma asked.

Rory pointed immediately.

Ma nodded with an impressed laugh. "How did you know?"

"Because he looks like the spitting image of Aaron." She looked up to see Cody watching her with the softest look in his eyes.

Rory gave him a shy, two-fingered wave, and he pulled a beer from a red cooler and canted his head in question.

"Get her one of those sweet ones I brought," Leah called out to him. "They're delicious. Taste just like strawberry lemonade, but get you a buzz."

"Oh, I shouldn't have anything to drink," Rory said, shaking her head. "I have Aaron..."

"Doesn't mean you can't enjoy the day, honey," Ma said. "He's fine. Look at him, and we'll all help watch those kiddos and keep them out of trouble. You don't have to overdo it, but Rory, it's okay to allow yourself to relax and have fun."

It felt good to have Ma say that. Since she was a

single mom, Rory had been hard on herself about being the perfect parent. But the reality was that she'd skipped her partying years. Did she regret it? Hell no. Aaron had kept her out of trouble. But she was twenty-five and had barely drank since that night with Cody because she'd been so scared that someone would look at her as inadequate. As if she had to make up for the one-night stand by being a robot.

Cody popped the top of a red drink and wiped the condensation on his shirt before he handed it to her. Leaning over her chair, gripping the plastic arm rests, he lowered his lips to her ear and whispered, "I won't drink. I'll watch our boy. Enjoy yourself." With a lingering kiss on her temple, he eased away and hopped up the porch stairs toward the grill Gage was manning.

Ma and Leah wore matching expressions of shock.

"Are you guys dating?" Ma asked.

"Or mating?" Leah asked, crossing her ankles on the grassy yard beneath them.

"Mating?" Rory asked, cheeks heating.

"Are you Cody's mate?" Leah leaned closer. "Dear

Lord, please say yes. I can't stand Shayna."

"Leah," Ma admonished.

"Admit it, Ma, she's rough to deal with. Too demanding and prissy."

Ma snorted and took a long pull of her fruit-flavored beer instead of answering. Finally, Ma asked, "Well, are you?"

"We're bonded," Rory admitted, dropping her gaze to the drink in her hands. "Does that make me his mate?"

Rory gasped when Leah pulled her into a lung-deflating hug, and Ma laughed a high pitched sound as she threw her arms around the both of them.

"Cody!" Ma yelled. "You mated, boy?"

Boone jerked his attention from where he was slathering sunscreen on Tate's arms. He stood with a big goofy grin on his face. "Aw, say it ain't so, Cody. You whooped?"

"Dammit," Cody murmured, but his grin was infectious as he escaped Gage's grip on his shoulder. "Well, I wanted to announce it after lunch. Come here, woman." He jerked his chin.

"Aaron," Rory called.

"Yeah, mommy?" the little boy asked from

behind Arie.

"Come here. Cody has something to tell you."

Aaron pumped his little legs and bounded up the porch steps in front of her. Cody threw him up in the air, and then pulled him close as his son giggled and squirmed. Hooking an arm over Rory's shoulder, he kissed the top of her hair as the Breck Crew gathered around, beers in hand as if they knew a toast was coming.

"Six years ago, I met this woman in a bar."

"So romantic," Boone called out.

"Shut it," Cody said with a laugh. "So six years ago, I was in a bad spot, you all remember. I saw this fiery, sassy redhead in a bar and thought, now that woman is one beautiful distraction."

Dade whistled a catcall and Rory giggled.

"When she left the next morning, I was wrecked, and I couldn't figure out why. A few days ago, that same redhead came back into my life, stormed it really, and brought me the best gift I've ever got." Cody's voice thickened as he dropped his eyes to Aaron, who was now clinging to his neck. "And I thought, man, life doesn't get better than this." Cody pressed his lips into Rory's hair again, as if he was trying to give himself a moment to compose himself. "But it did," he rasped out. "Because little did I know, that beautiful distraction I met in a bar all those years ago was going to turn out to be the best thing that ever happened to me. I'd met my mate. I just didn't know it at the time."

Rory smiled through twin tears that streamed down her face and snuggled against Cody's side, safe and warm next to her boys.

"Breck Crew," Boone called out. "Lift your drinks because today our family grew by two. Your alpha is bonded!"

Whistles and cheering filled the clearing. Bottles clinked, and the crew stormed the porch to embrace them.

Rory's heart was so full, tears of joy wet her face. Leah and Ma were crying, too, when they hugged her, and she melted against them. It felt so damned good to be accepted—to be enough for this family she respected so much.

"What did you have to tell *me*?" Aaron asked with a confused frown scrunching up his little freckle-laden nose.

Cody settled him on his feet and knelt in front of

him, gripping his small shoulders. “Do you want to stay in Breckenridge, buddy?”

Aaron lifted his gaze to Rory, and she nodded. “We can stay if you want to, baby.”

“Yes!” Aaron crowed, jumping up and down. “I want to. I want to go to Arie and Tate’s school and stay here with Daddy Cody. I mean Cody. And Aunt Leona and grandma, and I want to be a bear in the woods—” He clapped his hands over his mouth and his eyes went round.

“Look around,” Cody said low, tugging his little hand from his mouth. “These are your people, boy. You can talk about bears in front of them, but no one else, okay? You didn’t do anything wrong. Everyone here except for your mom has a bear inside of them.”

“They do?”

Cody nodded solemnly. “Big ones.”

“Tate and Arie, too, right?”

“They have bears just the same size as yours. You won’t have to feel scared of your animal anymore because we’re all going to teach you how to control that part of yourself, okay?”

“Can we go down the slide now?” Aaron asked.

“I think that’s a great idea,” Boone said, scooping

Rory up so fast she yelped.

Dade and Gage pulled Cody to his feet and bullied him down the porch stairs. Cody only fought them half-heartedly. He seemed to be laughing too hard to give it any real opposition as Aaron jumped up and down around them, pumping his tiny fists in the air in his signature victory dance.

"Boone, you put me down right now," Rory protested. "I wasn't planning on going down the slide."

"Then why'd you come in that swimsuit? Sorry, Rory. It's initiation day for the Breck Crew, and this is your moment." He looked down at her with his laughing blue eyes, so like Cody's. "Enjoy it," he whispered as he set her down at the top of the tarp and shoved her.

Cody hit the slide beside her, holding Aaron, giving that booming laugh with the dimples that said he was completely happy in this moment. Rory nearly glowed from the inside out as they picked up speed. Boone and Dade were yelling behind them as they slid down after them, followed by Tate and Arie and the others. A giant pile of werebears on a redneck Slip 'N Slide.

Rory flopped over and stretched out on her stomach, arms out for balance as she picked up enough speed to bottom out her stomach. She giggled breathlessly as Cody and Aaron slid around her, hooting about winning.

"Too slow, Dodson!" Boone called as he passed.

In her defense, these boys probably had a hundred pounds of muscle on her, and their weight was making them much more torpedo-like than she was.

At the bottom, she slid off the edge of the tarp and caught Arie before she could hit the grass. Laughter bubbled up her throat as she chased the Kellers back up the hill to go again. When she paused right before they made it to the top, Aaron bustled past her legs with his cousins.

Rory was soaking wet, covered in soap suds, her hair clung to her face, and her skin was sticky. And she'd never been happier in a single moment than she was right now.

Cody wrapped his arm around her waist and kissed her silly. With a cheek-splitting grin, one that nearly buckled her knees, he whispered, "I like when you look all happy like this."

His tattoos stood stark against the thin, soaking white T-shirt that still clung to his chest, and his defined pecs rose and fell under his steady breath. She gripped the wet fabric of his shirt and stood on her tiptoes. She left a kiss on his cheek, then wrapped her arms around his neck. He lifted her off her feet and rocked her gently, cupping the back of her head with his hand as if she was precious to him.

"Up on the porch you said I was the best thing to ever happen to you," she whispered.

"You are."

Those two words were said so confidently she hugged him even tighter.

Easing back, she cupped his neck and allowed him to see the honesty of her words. "I feel the same about you."

He searched her face as his dimples faded and his intense eyes softened. "Say it."

"Say what?" she teased.

"You know what."

"What if I want you to say it first?"

"I love you," he said on a breath, void of hesitation. "Always have. I just didn't have words to describe how deeply I felt about you until last night."

Against the palm of her hand, his face was smooth. It was invaluable, and she realized, in this moment, that Cody was necessary to her life now. He was a good man, a good father to her son, but more than that, he was everything she wanted. He made her feel complete and confident in herself. Where she'd felt weak and insecure for so long, he made her feel strong.

He was a firefighter, and his job was dangerous, but she would always be there, waiting for him to come home, her arms and heart open for him. It was risky, giving her soul to a man who could be taken from her so easily, but he was worth it. She'd rather have one day with Cody than a lifetime with a man she didn't burn for.

The words that tumbled from her lips were the easiest she'd ever said. "I love you back."

ELEVEN

Cody had that faraway look again as he sat slumped against one of the posts on the porch. He took a long pull on his bottled water, downing it, then crumpled the plastic before he dropped it beside him and went back to fingering what looked like the paperclip Aaron had given him.

Something had happened that had Cody pulling away slowly throughout the day. The lower the sun sank in the sky, the more withdrawn he became. Rory couldn't figure it out. She'd asked him three times what was wrong, but he'd plaster on a smile and kiss her. Then he'd murmur it was nothing—he had a lot on his mind.

The afternoon had been perfect, but as time had

worn on, he'd withdrawn into himself. Even his brothers were shooting each other worried looks.

Cody drew his knee up to his chest and stared out over his land, his eyes ghosting over where Rory sat beside Leah to Dade's jacked-up Ford pickup. In the bed, Boone had stacked blankets and draped a tarp over the top when the kids had gone sluggish. All three of the cubs were cuddled up asleep, the tarp protecting them from the late sunlight. A day of sliding, playing chase, eating, and swinging on the old tire out front had worn them out. Dade's truck played soft country songs as the rest of the Breck Crew sat around talking the hours away.

Rory tried to stay in the conversation, but Cody's change in mood kept her distracted and on edge.

He ran his hands over his hair, sighed and stood. He approached with a tired smile and pulled her out of the chair, then settled her into his lap. "I have to go somewhere tonight. I want you to stay here with Boone until I get back."

"What? No, I can just go back to Aunt Leona's house."

"I need you here with Boone. I can't explain why either. I just need you to trust me."

"You said no more," Ma said, her voice shaking with something Rory didn't understand. Fear? Anger? Perhaps both.

"What's going on?" Rory asked, twisting in his lap until she faced him.

Cody's hand gripped her thigh, and he brushed her hair off her shoulder. Exposing her neck, he stared at her collar bone and refused to meet her gaze. "I have something I have to do."

"This is fucked. You know that, right?" Dade asked.

"Yeah, well, this is our life," Cody said in a low, gravelly voice. "This is *my* life. Sometimes I have to do things we hate. Sometimes you all do, too. It's what keeps everyone breathing."

"How long?" Boone asked.

"How long what?"

"How long has he been pressing on you?" His voice cracked like a whip.

A muscle twitched under Cody's eye as he lifted a feral gaze to his brother. Something at the edge of Rory's senses thickened the air. Cody hadn't moved much, but suddenly, her instincts were screaming to get out of the way.

"Look, Cody," Gage said, hands out in a calming gesture. "At some point, we have to make our stand. This has gone on too long."

"What the hell is going on?" Rory asked again, louder this time as she scrambled out of Cody's lap to escape the suffocating feeling that clawed at the back of her throat. "What are you talking about?"

Cody let off a growl that lifted the hairs on her arm. He stood so fast the chair toppled over behind him. Without a word, he took the porch steps two at a time and disappeared inside.

"Why Boone?" Leah asked. "Rory and Aaron can stay with us."

"Because you already have too much to protect," Boone said in a defeated voice. His eyes were on the open doorway where Cody had disappeared. "If he fails—"

"He won't," Gage snarled.

"You don't even know what Krueger asked him to do," Dade said, standing. His eyes were two angry slits as he glared at Gage. "He's not invincible, big brother. You think he wanted to be alpha? You think he wants to deal with this shit alone? He's sacrificed enough. This *family* has sacrificed enough."

"Dade," Ma whispered as moisture filled her eyes.

"Don't, Ma. Don't pretend it doesn't gut you when you watch one of us forced into a dog fight. I'm going with him." Dade strode after Cody and slammed the door behind him.

Gage and Boone stood as one, but Ma slashed her hand through the air. "Sit down! Both of you. He's left you here for a reason. You'll keep our family safe while he buys us more time. Boone, he's given you his mate and his son to protect. Sit."

Rory didn't understand what was happening. Cody was going into danger. That much was clear. It didn't feel like a firefight, though. It felt like someone was forcing him to do something he didn't want to. To buy them time? What did that mean?

"Can you watch Aaron?" she asked Boone.

"Yeah," he answered, staring at his hands, "but I wouldn't go in there right now."

Ignoring him, she ran up the steps and threw the door open. Following the quiet murmurs of the Keller brothers, she found herself in the door frame of Cody's bedroom, the room they'd shared last night.

Across the bed was a belt with three different

sized knives. It looked military, and she gasped as her eyes landed on the camo gun case. Cody was already clad in black cargo pants and a tight T-shirt in the same shadowy color.

"I want to know where you're going." Damn her voice as it shook.

Cody cast her a glance over his shoulder as he pulled a black duffle bag from the closet. "I can't tell you."

"Why?"

Dade pulled on his own black T-shirt over a large puckered scar on his back. "Because he can't. He's not allowed to."

Rory crossed her arms. They pulled on belts and shoved knives into sheaths as if they'd prepared for battle a hundred times before. Hell, maybe they had.

"Is what you're doing illegal?"

Cody huffed a humorless sound and shook his head. "The people who give me orders are above the law."

"Is what you're doing dangerous?"

Cody pulled the strap of the duffle bag over his chest as Dade pulled the long-range weapon's case off the bed.

Her mate stepped in front of her and ran his fingers through her hair until his palm cupped her cheek. "Less dangerous than the alternative."

"Which is?"

Cody shook his head, apology written all over his face. "We'll be back by morning." His voice sounded strange, forced, when he said those words.

She gripped his hand, desperate to keep his touch on her cheek. "Why do I get the feeling you're telling me goodbye, just in case?" And why did she suddenly get the feeling that being a firefighter wasn't the riskiest part of Cody's life?

Cody pulled her hand to his lips and kissed her knuckles softly. "I just got you and Aaron back." Determination lifted his eyebrows as he leveled her with a look. "I'll come back. Always."

He sidled around her, and she followed him and Dade out the front door. Leaning against the railing of the porch, she watched Cody stride toward the truck where Aaron was still sleeping near his cousins. He whispered something too low for her to make out, then leaned into the truck bed and kissed the cowlick on top of Aaron's blond head. Turning, he hugged the Breck Crew roughly, one by one, spending more time with Ma. And when he was finished, Cody graced Rory with one more look, then hopped in his truck.

When Dade was settled on the passenger's side, Cody pulled away, leaving a deep and echoing emptiness in the pit of Rory's chest.

Cody was leaving her here to do something precarious—something that could hurt him, or worse.

And on top of that, he hadn't trusted her enough to let her into that part of his life.

He'd seemed so open last night, so happy about their bond, but when it came to the real grit that held two people together, he wasn't interested in forsaking his bachelor ways. Was this how it was going to be? She would only have the parts of him he wanted her to see? The pretty pieces—the summer memories, easy words, and smiles. That's not what she wanted. Rory was in this, ready to give all of herself, but the man she'd been destined for couldn't give her the same.

Agony congealed her blood, making it hard to move her arms and legs as she swallowed a sob down. Her chest burned like a tiny flame where his touch and gentle affection had sealed their bond. As she stared out over the pink and orange streaks across the evening sky, a tear slipped down her cheek and made a small *splat* against the railing of the porch.

She'd bonded to a man incapable of letting her in.

TWELVE

"What's that?" Dade asked.

Cody fingered the little paperclip between his fingers and looked up at his youngest brother sitting across the chopper from him. "My boy gave it to me the first time I met him." Leaning back, Cody stuffed the memento deep into his pocket and pulled a bulletproof vest over his torso. "Something feels off," he said in a low voice the pilot would miss.

Sure, the pick-up point had been the same, the chopper had been waiting, and the pilot was the same one who took him on all the missions Krueger recruited him for, but still—something niggled at the edges of his instincts.

Dade shook his head and strapped himself into

his own bulletproof vest. "Just focus on what we have to do. Let's just get in and out of there. Krueger gave us all the instructions, and it seems like a cut-and-clear kill."

Kill. That word awoke his bear, and he closed his eyes against the urge to let the animal have his body.

When the chopper began its descent, Cody pulled the gun case from under his seat to the floor in front of him. Preparing and building the long-range weapon was second nature after his time in the war, and by the time he screwed on the silencer, his mind was on its way to being right again. There wasn't time to think about the reasons why the mission felt off, especially when he hadn't been able to come up with a single reason why. It was probably just Rory in his head. By morning, he would have to face her with blood on his hands. Sure, his targets were always terrorists, but by nature, he wasn't a killer. He was a protector. He'd have to hide this side of his life for always if he wanted to keep her and Aaron.

But Dade was right. Get his head on straight, find the target, neutralize the threat, go home, and hope his overburdened soul could bear the life he'd taken. Hope Rory saw him as more than just some attack dog on a short leash.

The sound of the chopper blades was deafening as they hit the ground. Meadow grass waved like an ocean against the sand, and he and Dade slipped out and nodded to the pilot. He was young, twenty-one, if that. Krueger must really trust him if he was his go-to chauffeur in all of this. His name badge read *Allen*, but the word was close enough to Aaron to make Cody wince.

Dade ran in front of him, low to the ground, eyes on a GPS unit that would lead them to the exact coordinates of the cabin the target had apparently chosen to hole up in. His brother had always been less emotional about this part of their lives—the hidden, bloody, gritty part that they kept from everyone outside of the Breck Crew.

The evergreen woods were quiet and doused in the blue light of a half moon. There were no clouds, no bird song, no little critters' heartbeats thumping in fear as he and Dade ran past. All was still except for the soft *pat-pat-pat* of the chopper blades fading behind them. Two miles of winding deer paths, jutting boulders, tripping vines, and shallow creek beds, and finally the scent of a man wafted to Cody on the breeze.

The wind kicked up suddenly, brushing this way and that against Cody's skin. *Go back*, it seemed to say. *Save your soul from this. Save Rory and Aaron from what you are becoming.*

Slapping his neck to rid himself of the chills there, he crouched down beside Dade on the edge of a tree line that surrounded a dilapidated cabin.

Probably only one room. The sealant between the logs had failed sometime in the home's history, likely allowing the elements and bugs inside. Half of the roof had caved in, and the front door was only attached by the bottom hinge so it hung lopsided over the frame.

A soft glowing light flickered from inside, and a shadow paced across the single window.

With a steadying breath, Cody dropped down to his belly and pulled down the spiked feet of the sniper rifle to prop it up. Securing his shoulder in place and resting his finger on the cold metal of the gun above the trigger, he closed one eye and looked through the scope.

The window was smeared with dirt, but he could make out a man inside. It would be an easy shot from here. He'd made a hundred others at targets much farther away, but as a soft voice drifted to him, he hesitated.

"What are you waiting for?" Dade asked in a voice as soft as a gentle breeze.

"Listen."

"To what. Let's just get this done so Krueger doesn't skin us."

Cody cast him a warning glance. "Dade, stop. Just listen."

His brother clenched his jaw but turned an ear to the decaying house.

The target was talking on the phone to someone, low enough that human ears wouldn't be able to make out his words from this distance, but Cody wasn't human.

"Maria, don't come out here. There is nothing you can do, and I need to know that you're safe. No, I swear I will. I can't have Krueger finding out about you. We've got this far keeping us a secret." The man paused in front of the window. "Babe, everyone is gone, and I can't offer you protection anymore." The man's voice cracked. "I think he'll send the Kellers. Babe, stop. Please stop crying."

Dade's eyes went wide, and he mouthed, *What the fuck?*

"That was stupid to say. I was only trying to tell you that they'll make it fast. No pain." The man's voice came out an agonized whisper as he said, "Maria. If I can't make it back to you, I want you to move on."

After that, the man took his time saying goodbye to a woman he obviously loved, and Dade continued to stare at Cody with that horrified expression that was probably mirrored on his own face right now. They'd never killed a target they knew had a girl waiting back home. Listening to that conversation had ripped the title *target* away from this man completely. He was a person who was scared and trying to console a woman who obviously cared deeply for him.

And how the fuck did he know the Kellers were coming? Or about Krueger?

The feeling of wrongness in his gut turned septic, and Cody shot upward to avoid getting sick in the ferns and leaving evidence of his presence here. "I'm going to talk to him."

"What?" Dade whisper-screamed.

Cody removed the ammo and clicked the safety on the weapon, then pulled his handgun. "I'm sure as fuck not going to kill someone who doesn't strike me as a terrorist. I don't want to kill blind, Dade."

"Ssshit," his brother hissed, following behind him. The crack of metal as Dade cocked his own handgun was too loud in the still night.

The man had disappeared from the window, and when Cody did a three-count on his fingers and kicked in the door, it became clear why.

The target had heard them coming.

Angry, feral eyes flashed in the lantern light as the silver of a blade arced toward Cody's throat. He ducked and rammed him backward until they hit a wall. The wood groaned under the impact but held. Cody dropped his gun and hit the man across the face. Bucking him off, the man threw a leg around the backs of his knees and landed Cody on his ass a split second before he was on him.

He blocked another slash of the knife. Where the fuck was Dade? A quick glance, and he could see Dade leaning against the wall, watching the fight with a look of utter confusion.

This target had fight training. That much was

clear from the two jaw-smashing punches he landed on Cody's face. The man lifted him and slammed him against the dining table with a splintering crash. Cody blocked and blocked again but was trying not to hurt the man.

Cody had questions, and dead people didn't talk.

But when the man sunk his serrated knife deeply into Cody's shoulder, red rage blasted through him as pain singed up his nerve endings. With a bellow of fury, he grabbed the man by his jacket and threw him against the wall, shattering the rotted logs completely and bringing part of the weakened roof on top of the target.

With a snarl, he slid the knife from his shoulder. Iron-scented warmth trickled out in spurts to the rhythm of his racing pulse. Hatred washed over him as he turned the hilt in his hand and bent down to grab the strip of jacket he could see in the rubble. The man's body crumpled in on itself and he groaned as Cody pulled him from the wreckage.

He smelled it then, in the exact moment the man dragged defeated looking, silver eyes to his. Fur.

Cody staggered backward, releasing his grip on the man's clothing. "What are you?"

The man huffed a breath. “What am I? I’m your mark, right? You’re a Keller, the government enforcer sent to snuff out the shifters they’ve lost control of.” The man spat. “Traitor.”

“What are you talking about?” Dade asked as he knelt down beside the man. “We aren’t enforcers.”

When the man smiled, his teeth were covered in red. “Fuck you.”

“You said Krueger’s name. How do you know him?” Cody asked, his stomach sinking with every second.

“Krueger was my handler. He was the handler for my entire crew. Five bears, and I’m the only one left. Bet you can’t guess why,” the shifter ground out. His dark hair was disheveled, and blood ran a river down the side of his face.

“I don’t understand,” Cody rasped out. “Why would Krueger kill your crew?”

The man shook his head slowly with an empty smile stretched across his face. His breath came in pants now, and he rattled when he breathed. “You don’t get it, do you? He uses you to put down the bears he’s lost control of. Those of us who resist doing his bidding, he deactivates. And for those of us who remove the trackers"—the man stretched his neck and showed an angry red scar where Krueger placed their tracking devices—"he sends in the Kellers."

"No," Cody said, standing and running his hands over his hair. "We were targeting terrorists."

"Krueger has lots of terms for our kind. Terrorist is his favorite."

"What's your name," Dade asked. "What Crew?"

"Adam Mercer of the late Bloodraid Crew. I'm all that's left."

"You and Maria," Dade said.

"No," Mercer breathed, the hatred falling from his face. "Please, she's not part of this. She's human. Please, man." The silver faded from his eyes, and the scent of fear filled the room. "Don't hurt her."

"We won't harm your woman," Dade said low. "I mean, fuck, we didn't even know we were hurting shifters. Krueger has been threatening our crew with this shit, too. It's why we do this. Killing isn't our choice." He dragged a tortured gaze to Cody. "Nothing is our choice."

No, no, no. They'd been killing shifters? Their own kind, and for what? Because those people hadn't done what Krueger wanted? Fuck! The people he had killed had cared for families once. They'd been innocent and not a risk to the American public at all. Not like Krueger had said.

If Krueger had done this to other crews, he was capable of wiping out the entire Breck Crew. He could hurt Rory and Aaron. Cody dropped to his knees beside the man and raised his knife. Mercer's eyes went wide as his gaze followed the arc of the blade. He screamed in pain as it sank deeply into his arm.

Panting, Mercer stared down at the injury as Cody ripped the metal out. "What are you doing?"

"Saving you," he growled out. "Bleed for a few minutes as you run through the woods, then cover your trail. We'll buy you time, but you and Maria need to disappear until we can figure out how to get rid of Krueger. Lay low somewhere safe where no one can recognize you."

"Okay," he gasped, nodding his head. "I will."

Dade dragged his gaze from Cody to Mercer. "You need to leave your ride here and ditch that cell phone. Call Maria from a payphone to meet up. Go now. You need as much of a head start as you can get."

Mercer ripped off his jacket and limped onto the front porch, dripping red from his fingertips. He turned at the frame. "Thank you," he said on a breath. "A bit of friendly advice since you spared my life—if I were you, I'd check your house thoroughly. Kruger places bugs. No video, just audio, but it's how he tells when he's losing control of a crew." He gave one last nod of gratitude before he spun and ran for the woods.

Cody couldn't see anything beyond Krueger's soul-shattering betrayal. He'd used them to kill their own kind. Used them in a human war they had no stake in. He'd threatened Cody's family and crew, and if what Mercer had said was true, someday, when they weren't useful to Krueger anymore, he'd kill them, too.

Boiling rage heated his blood, burning through him until his bear was just beneath his surface.

"Fuck," Dade whispered. "What are we going to do?"

Cody looked from the blood-smattered rubble to his brother. "We're going hunting."

"For what?"

"For Krueger."

THIRTEEN

Rory startled awake. It was dark in the guest bedroom, and she cuddled Aaron closer against her. Chills rippled up her skin from a nightmare she couldn't quite remember. The air was thick with something that prickled the back of her neck, and the scent of iron clung to the air particles like a fog.

"Cody?" she whispered, unsure why his name would even register on her lips.

"I'm here," came a voice so deep and growly she didn't recognize it.

Fear pulsed through her veins, forcing her to act or she'd scream. She sat straight up. "Where are you?"

A shadow shifted under the window, and she

gasped. Blue moonlight illuminated a crouched figure, eyes glowing with an animal reflection she saw from raccoons and stray dogs on night roads.

"Cody, I can't see very well." Her voice quivered and she hated how scared she sounded. "Can we turn on the light?"

"Best we don't. I just wanted to see you. Go back to sleep, Rory. We'll talk in the morning."

The hell they would. She kicked out of the covers and followed him out, the oversize T-shirt she'd swiped from his drawer billowing around her knees. The door clicked closed behind her, and when she turned, the soft light from the kitchen showed a terrifying figure. Cody was in a man's body, but his face had morphed into an expression she didn't recognize. He was wild and shook with barely checked rage, or agony, or both.

His black T-shirt was ripped down the arm, and red followed a bulging vein down his bicep and pooled in the crease at his elbow before the stream continued down to his fingertips. Blood had splattered up his neck, and his eyes weren't the muddy brown and green that indicated his animal was fighting for control. They were bright gold.

His Adam's apple dipped low as he swallowed. Straightening his spine, he looked down at her as if he was daring her to hold his gaze. She couldn't. Not even for a second.

He arced his attention to the couch where Boone was sitting with his hands clasped over his knees. "I'm calling a Crew meeting. No phones. I'll meet you at Ma's at dawn, and I want everyone there."

Hair mussed from what appeared to be a restless sleep, or none at all, Boone nodded and pulled on his shirt that was lying crumpled on the floor beside the couch. He murmured his goodbye to Rory, then let himself out the front door.

"What happened?" she whispered.

Cody clicked his tongue against his teeth and turned for his room, leaving her to trail after him.

"What's happened is I've found a safe house for you in Wyoming. I have a half-brother named Bruiser there, and his crew can protect you."

"His crew?"

"You'll stay with the Ashe Crew until I send for you. You and Aaron will be safe there. They have protection from a shifter named Damon Daye, and Bruiser will keep you safe—"

"Stop it! I'm not going anywhere until you tell me what is going on. I brought Aaron to you because it was safer than being out in the world alone, not knowing who to trust. And now you're sending me to a stranger—"

"Not a stranger. He's family."

"I didn't even know you had a half-brother, Cody! I've been left out of all of this, and for what? Why are you hiding from me?"

Cody shook his head and let off a snarl, then strode into the bathroom and pulled his shirt over his head. The man didn't even wince at the deep slice in his arm, which gushed with his movement.

"Why?" She leaned on the frame and waited. "Why, Cody? I'm not going to quit asking until you give me a fucking answer. I'm not leaving for some safe house if that means we're split up and you are at risk."

"We're all at risk, Rory. Every one of my Crew is in danger, and I can't keep my head if you are here. If Aaron is here."

"What am I running from? You owe me that much, at least. Give me anything, Cody. Give me something. Please."

Cody closed his eyes against his reflection in the mirror. He cut her an anguished look and held it. "You're too good for this. Too good for me. I'm dark inside, and I've done awful things. Things that will taint you and Aaron."

"Tell me." Her voice trembled like a branch in a storm, but fuck it all. Gritting her teeth, she tried again, louder and stronger. "Tell me, Cody. If you keep pushing me away, I definitely won't stand for that shit. At least if you share your life with me, we have a shot at being okay. I'm not fragile, and your secrets won't break me. I know you think you're protecting me by throwing up walls I don't have the tools to batter down, but you aren't. You're hurting me."

Cody swallowed hard and crouched down, holding onto the sink as his long legs folded beneath him. An anguished sound wrenched from his throat. "You'll leave me."

"Cody, you are good. I can see it. You're a good man who loves his family and protects his own. Spill whatever is hurting you, and let me share the burden. Let me in."

"I killed them," he said so softly, she almost

missed it.

"What? Killed who?"

"My own kind. A dozen marks. They weren't terrorists."

Rory shook her head slowly as dread filled her stomach and made her limbs too heavy to move. Slowly, she fell to her knees beside him, the tile unforgiving against her shins.

"The government has an agency who handles my kind. Shifters. The International Exchange of Supernatural Affairs has a leader, a handler, and he's the one who sanctioned my tours in the war."

"I don't understand. The government made you fight?"

Cody sat hard, resting his back against the bathtub, and drew his knee to his chest, as if it would protect him from the heartbreaking admissions coming from his lips. He reached deep in his pocket and pulled out a small plastic bag of what looked like electronic pieces that had been smashed to bits. "I found these in my bedroom and in the living room. They're bugs. Sound only, but we've been monitored, and I have no idea when my handler, Krueger, had them placed. I do missions for him. Black ops terrorist sniper shit that he needs someone with my abilities to do. My brothers have been recruited, too, but the bulk of the marks are given to me. He told me my targets were terrorists, but tonight, Dade and I talked to the mark. He was a shifter, Rory. Another bear whose entire crew had been wiped out, and I almost pulled the trigger on him."

"But you didn't—"

"But I have! A dozen other times I killed shifters who didn't deserve it. They just weren't buying Krueger's bullshit anymore, and he used me to end them. Their blood is on my hands."

"Cody, how could you have known? How?"

"I shouldn't have taken missions blind like I did. I trusted him too much and got desperate to save my own people. I didn't ask enough questions."

"What did he hold over you?"

"Exposure. Public registration for shifters. And lately he has been threatening my family's safety. And then when you came along..." Cody swallowed hard and looked ill, shook his head slowly from side to side. "Krueger knows about you and Aaron."

"What?" she whispered. Her face tingled as the blood drained from it.

"He knows Aaron is my kid."

"Does he know he's a bear shifter?"

Cody nodded but wouldn't meet her eye. "It would've been safer for you and him if you had never come back."

"How can you say that?"

"Because he wants him tagged, Rory! This," he said, stretching his neck to expose a short, surgically straight scar that ran along the taut muscle, "is where my tracking device was placed. Gage, Dade, Boone, Leah, Ma…even the cubs have them, Rory. This is part of the control. This is our leash. When I had a meeting the other day, it was to get my instructions for this mission, and Krueger said he wanted me to bring Aaron in for his tag."

"He calls it tagging?"

"Yeah. That's what it is, right? I'm an animal who needs to be controlled in the unsuspecting public." The words sounded bitter and filled with self-loathing.

"Fuck that, Cody. Krueger is the animal. Our son isn't having some tracker put in him. Over my cold, rotting corpse will that ever happen."

"Yeah, that's what I told him, too. He's not

budging on it, though, and I wouldn't put it past him to snatch you and Aaron when I'm not looking and force the tracker on him." Cody pressed the heels of his palms against his closed eyes and muttered a curse. "Everything got so messed up, and just as you came into my life. It shouldn't be like this."

"No, Cody. Things were really messed up before we came. You just have more to protect now, so it feels bigger. What do we do?"

"*We* don't do anything. You'll go to Wyoming while I figure out a way to neutralize the threat."

"I'm not leaving."

Cody jerked his gaze to her and leveled her with a glare. "Yes, you will."

"Sorry, sexy. Your dominant alpha shit isn't going to work on me. I'm not a bear, remember? You want to boss people around, go push your super bear powers on the other shifters who feel a need to bow down to you. I'm not leaving you. Aaron and I are safest here, with you and the rest of the Breck Crew, as a family."

Cody's face went slack. His shocked expression would have been funny if not for the very un-hilarious situation they'd found themselves in. And if his eyes weren't blazing like a demon's.

She'd seen a ton of spy movies, and the reality of their situation was that a bag of real-life shattered bugs was sitting on the tile in front of her and her mate had been a working assassin for a government program that didn't give a shit about his welfare or the welfare of shifters who wouldn't do their bidding. The reality was that she'd stepped tits first into a secret government program that was taking advantage of a group of supernatural beings who were trying desperately to keep to the fringes of society. She could only imagine what humans would do if they ever found out shifters existed. She'd imagined a hundred horrifying scenarios in the years that she had raised Aaron alone.

But could she take Aaron and run from the man whom she felt safest with? From the father of her son and the one she'd given her heart to? Could she run from Aaron's only shot at normalcy?

She'd be in the wind again, this time with strangers, and with the knowledge that the people she feared the most already knew about Aaron and what he was. They'd be hunted, always looking over their shoulders and always waiting for a phone call on Cody's fate.

No, she was done running. Done hiding and fearing the life she'd been thrust into. She thought of Leah and Ma. Of the Keller brothers who'd accepted her completely as mate of their alpha. As family. She couldn't turn her back on them and run, knowing it wasn't any safer out there than right here with people who cared about she and Aaron's welfare.

Half-brother or not, a stranger wouldn't have the instinct to protect Aaron. Not like Cody.

"I know you'll drag the ghosts of your targets to the grave. It's the way you are, Cody," she whispered. "But I'm going to be here, fighting alongside you to avenge the people you were tricked into hurting."

"Not hurting, Rory. Killing. I killed them. I put the scope to their heads, pulled a trigger, and left their bodies for a clean-up crew to take care of. It doesn't matter that Krueger betrayed us. All that matters is that they are lying in a shallow grave or a lab somewhere because I wasn't strong enough to tell Krueger to fuck off."

"And if you had?"

"He would've killed my family." Cody said it void of hesitation. "But what makes me or my people any more important than the ones Krueger ordered a hit on?"

Tears burned her eyes as she witnessed the pain that flashed across Cody's face.

"As long as I live, I'll be tainted. My bear has been damaged by years of war and violence, and I'll never be a good mate for you or father for Aaron. How can I look my boy in the eye and try and teach him to be a good man when I'm a murderer?"

"Stop it," she ground out, dashing moisture from her eyes with her fingertips. "Stop talking like that. You didn't know. You were used and threatened, and you didn't know. All you can do now is avenge them."

"And I will." He hooked his hands around his knee and leaned back. "The Breck Crew is about to go to war with a man who has never lost a battle against us. And when I think of anything happening to you or to Aaron..." His voice cracked on his son's name. He shook his head and dropped his gaze. "I never wanted any of this."

Swallowing down her heartache at seeing what Krueger had leached from the man she loved, Rory stood and busied herself with warming tap water in the sink, then moistening a dark washrag she dug from the linen closet. Straddling his lap, she kissed the short stubble on his cheek, then began to wash away the blood on his arm. The cut looked deep, but already the layers of muscle were sealing together, leaving a slightly raised scar under the skin that had been laid open. Aaron could heal from a scraped knee in minutes, but the ability shifters had to recover never ceased to amaze her.

Cody's face never changed. He never winced away from her touch. He only stared at the wall beside him and held perfectly still. His nostrils flared. He angled his face, then lifted his supernatural gaze to hers. "You're afraid of me now. I can smell it."

"You smell fear, but it isn't for you. I'm scared of what will happen now. I'm scared you'll be hurt, that Aaron will be tagged, and that I won't be able to save either of you."

"It's not your responsibility to save us."

"Why not? You're my mate. I love you."

Cody gripped her hand, stilling the gentle washing motion against his arm. "Say that again."

"I've always loved you, and even after what you told me, I love you still. You are the father of my child, and how could I not feel a bone-deep devotion to you? Even when I didn't know you, my heart was yours. And now that I do, my soul is yours, too."

"You'd give your soul to a man like me?"

"Yes," she said on a sigh. Resting her forehead against his, she murmured, "To a *good* man like you. The targets you were forced into… I know what that will do to you. I can see it, but I'll be here, carrying those scars with you. Just don't shut me out anymore. I'm not running, Cody. I'm part of this crew, too. I'll be there when the pain of what you've done buckles you, and I'll be standing quietly behind you when you exact your revenge on Krueger in the name of all of those people and families he has hurt."

"It's not just Krueger, though. He'll be a cockroach. Kill one, and there will be another just like him to take his place. If I do this, we're going to war with the IESA."

Rory was scared. Dear Lord, those words terrified her worse than she'd ever been before. But if anyone was strong enough to put an end to Krueger's cruelty, it was her mate. Cody was capable and protective with a hard-wired moral compass with an arrow stuck on doing what was right over doing what was easy.

She huffed a sigh and leaned against his chest, folding her arms in between them until he surrounded her with his strong embrace like a cocoon. Whatever was coming their way, she was in this now, like it or not.

Under her, Cody's muscles twitched and shook. His erection had grown hard and long, pressing against the material of his black cargo pants until she could see the perfect outline.

"I need..." His breath came out in pants, and the room began to smell like animal fur.

"Shh. It's okay," she whispered against his ear, fighting the fear of being too near when he was this close to a Change.

He wouldn't hurt her. He wouldn't.

Slowly, she rolled her hips against his lap and sucked gently on his ear. A long, low growl resonated from his chest. Trailing kisses down his neck, she ran her fingernails down his chest as his breath sped up. His hands grasped her hips and dragged her against his erection as a low groan escaped his lips, interrupting the rumbling sound in his throat.

Her stomach dipped as he pulled her upward and covered her mouth with his own. If his injury hurt, he didn't show it as he lifted her off the ground and squeezed her to his chest. Walking slowly, he backed her into his room toward the bed. Rotating her, he lay down, propped against the headboard. He pulled her knees on the soft comforter on either side of his waist. She pushed her tongue past his lips and tasted him.

"Fffuck," he murmured as she eased away, thrusting his hips against her like he couldn't help himself.

His stomach flexed, mounds of muscle growing tight with every breath he drew. He pulled her shirt over her head and his skin crashed against hers. His hands were everywhere, running the length of her back, around the curve of her ass, down the back of her thighs to the crease behind her knees where he pulled her closer still. She pressed her hands on his abs that hardened with every powerful thrust of his hips against her.

The thin material of her panties was soaking now. She directed his hand against the moisture there.

Cody angled his face and kissed her deeply, his jaw working with each stroke of his tongue against hers. His hips moved rhythmically against her, the pressure building from his stony shaft that pressed against her clit.

"I'm coming," she whispered, arching her back as a deep pulsing orgasm rocketed through her.

Cody's teeth grazed her neck as a ripping sound filled the air. He tossed her panties away, and his finger sank into her in time to feel the aftershocks while she rubbed against his touch. Before she was recovered, she pulled at the button of his pants and unzipped him, then shimmed the dirt-stained material from his legs. He lay there, pliable under her touch, black briefs clinging to his powerful thighs, stomach flexing as he stared at her breasts with the neediest expression she'd ever seen.

"You want to taste?" she asked, her voice husky.

He nodded, pupils dilated so that only a thin ring of gold shone from his eyes in the dim light from the bathroom.

"Me first." She pulled at the elastic of his briefs and unsheathed the swollen head of his cock. Then she pulled the material down his legs and tossed it in a pile on the floor. She lapped up the drop of creamy moisture that sat at the tip of his shaft. Cody gave a sharp inhalation of breath and leaned his shoulder blades back against the headboard. Winding his fingers in her hair, he guided her back to him and spread his legs, allowing her into the space between. Back arched, she took him in her mouth and circled his head with her tongue, then released him.

"Rory," he pleaded in a strained whisper.

With a smile at how empowered she felt at getting a dominant apex predator alpha like Cody to beg, she gripped the base of his shaft and took him into her mouth again deeper. He was trying to keep his hands gentle in her hair, she could tell, but he was losing control as she dragged it out, stroking him slowly.

"Ass in the air for me, love," he said, and she obliged, knees spread wide on the bed.

He was groaning now, a soft little noise every time she lowered her mouth over him. God, she loved when he was like this. On the edge of his control, trying to be gentle, allowing her to lead.

He'd witnessed horrors and been forced to do unimaginable things, but here, for a little while, she could make him forget. She could give his heart a rest from carrying the burdens of his position in the crew.

He was bucking into her mouth faster now, fingers tightening in her hair, a soft rumbling sound emanating from his chest. "Stop," he demanded in a gravelly voice. "I want to finish in you."

With a smile, she turned away from him. Over her shoulder, she watched his look of absolute focus as she offered him her body. On her hands and knees, she panted in anticipation as he stroked his long, thick shaft with his hand. Gracefully, he splayed his knees behind her and pulled his hand between her legs, brushing her from quivering belly to wet seam. He pressed two fingers deep inside of her, and his breath caught there in the quiet room.

"You're always so wet when I need you to be," he said, and she smiled at the praise.

He pulled his hand away and pushed the head of his cock inside her. She arched her back and rolled her eyes closed at how good he felt inside. Propping herself on one arm, she pressed her fingers on either side of her entrance and felt him slide into her again. He went deeper this time, and she moaned his name as she touched her clit.

Cody leaned on one arm, his bicep bulging beside her as he reached under her and kneaded her breast.

He kissed her shoulder blade as he pushed into her again, then pulled out. She backed up against him the next time, taking all of him, and his control faltered. His strokes filled her faster and faster until his slick cock rubbed constantly between her fingers. She was gone now, off in space somewhere as another orgasm crashed through her. Cody slammed into her, a snarl rattling his chest as his powerful hips hit her backside over and over again. She spread her knees wider to feel more of him, and Cody froze, then thrust again hard. Wetness shot into her and trickled down her thighs as Cody swelled and released into her.

She sank onto her elbows as his movement slowed and he pulsed along with her. Reverently, he rubbed her back and trailed kisses down her spine as he moved inside of her until soft tingling filled her again.

The last orgasm, he drew from her gently. His name was soft against her lips as she came again.

"What are you doing to me?" he whispered against her neck.

Rory huffed a soft laugh as he eased out and pulled her against his chest. She felt so safe and warm in his arms. "This is me telling you I'm not afraid of you or this life. I'm not going anywhere."

His fingertip brushed her skin as he dragged it along the curve of her waist to her hip, then back up again. "So this is your decision then. You'll stay with me?"

She sighed and snuggled closer against him. "Always."

FOURTEEN

Cody nodded a greeting to Boone who was currently checking off supplies in the back of the ambulance that sat next to Engine 4. A big part of this job was making sure they were prepared for anything, which meant checking that everything was working and ready at the beginning of each shift. Dade was hosing down the engine, clad in a uniform that matched Cody's exactly. Blue pants to match the blue fire department shirt and thick-soled boots. If Shayna called in from dispatch with an emergency, they'd change quick as a whip into their protective gear.

Hefting his duffle bag over his shoulder, Cody shoved open the heavy metal door that led down the hallway to the rooms. His was the third on the right. He shared it with a rookie hire from Fairplay who'd been with the department for just a few months. Cody pushed open the door to his room and stopped dead in his tracks.

Shayna sat on the bed, elbows locked and knees spread suggestively. Her skirt was midway up her thigh and gave him a peek at the bright pink sheer panties she was wearing.

"What do you want?" he asked, not in the mood for games. He set his duffle bag on a chair beside the bed and shot her an irritated glare.

"You know what I want."

"How did you even get in here?" Because really, if she'd snuck past both of his brothers without them noticing, he was going to give them hell about using their damned shifter senses better. And surely they would've given him a warning if they knew she was in here waiting for him. His brothers seemed to be die-hard Rory fans since she'd come back into his life.

"We could've been great," she murmured, canting her head. Her dark eyes were cold and lifeless as she raked her gaze over him. "But then you went and got your little whore knocked up, didn't you? I was on the fast track to a promotion because of my relationship with you, but you had to go and fuck everything up, didn't you?"

Promotion? Cody narrowed his eyes at the seductress on the bed. Couldn't be. There was no way Shayna was IESA. She was too impatient to put in years like that chasing him for a job.

"Are you putting it all together, big boy?"

"Get out," he growled. "Now."

"Now wait a minute. I came here on a mission. Less violent than the missions you've been acing. I'm not a killer. But my job is just as important. I'm intel, and right now I'm doubling as sexy messenger maiden. I'm here to give you your next instructions." With two splayed fingers, she pushed a thick folder the color of baby puke toward him on the bed.

He snatched it and pulled a stack of papers from it. The first page was a picture of Rory and Aaron playing at a park he didn't recognize. The next was of them entering an apartment building, and the next showed them sitting on a bench, as if they were waiting for a bus.

"They were never really safe, Cody," Shayna purred. "Krueger wants your son tagged. He's a

Keller, and your bloodline is important to this program. And we know that he'll grow up a ticking time bomb just like his old man, so for the safety of the public, he needs a tracker. There are instructions on the next page on where to meet."

"And if I refuse?"

Shayna giggled and dipped her chin. "Oh, Cody. You know you're replaceable, right? Your entire family is. Especially after that botched mission. Krueger is not happy that you missed the target and then lost him in the woods." Shayna made a sympathetic clicking sound. "You're skating on thin ice, Keller. Our program is only interested in operators who are of use to us." Shayna spread her knees wider and smiled wickedly. Pulling her panties to the side, she pressed a red-clawed finger inside of herself with a wet sound and a practiced-sounding groan. Never taking her eyes from him, she whispered, "You want to have a fuck?"

Cody swallowed down his disgust and focused on a seam in the concrete wall. He'd never been with her, and seeing her like this after being with Rory made his stomach churn.

"Suit yourself." Shayna pouted her heavily

glossed lips. "Pity really. You could've been a good lay for a big dumb bear. Have a nice rest of your life, Keller. Oh," she said, standing to leave. "If I were you, I'd do everything just right if you want to live through the week. If you haven't noticed, Krueger isn't a patient man." Shayna's low snicker echoed down the hallway as she left.

Cody slumped onto the bed. There had to be fifty pictures of Rory and Aaron, and the one at the bottom of the pile had been taken when his son was around a year old. Cody touched the boy's smiling face with the tip of his finger and closed his eyes.

Using Aaron as bait was the last thing in the world he wanted to do, but what choice did he have? Krueger had injected all of the Keller's with trackers, and this might be his only shot at drawing him into the open.

His instincts screamed to get Rory and Aaron as far away from here as possible, but he couldn't. Slow simmering fury burned through his body as he thought of Krueger forcing a tracker in Aaron. Rory had been right. They were safest with him, where his seething bear wanted to kill everything that threatened them.

He read the instructions for the meeting and clutched the paper hard in his clenched fist.

In two days' time, Krueger would push Cody's bear too far. He had to know he was cornering a predator bent on protecting his young, but apparently the asshole thought his position in IESA put him above consequences.

In two days' time, Krueger would try to hurt his boy.

Cody stared at the pictures, and his bear shredded and raged under the surface at the idea that Krueger had followed his family before he'd even known them.

Two more days, and Cody was going to burn Krueger and his entire fucking program to the ground.

****

Rory knew the plan, had memorized and gone over it with the Breck Crew in the meeting yesterday, but it still didn't sit well with her that she and Aaron would be the bait to draw a soulless man like Krueger in. It also didn't help that Cody was on a two-day shift at the fire station right now. Things always seemed clearer when he was around, instilling confidence in her that he'd never let anything happen to Aaron.

She suddenly got the feeling that she was a diver treading shark infested waters without a cage.

"Are you okay, dear?" Aunt Leona asked. "You seem so distracted this morning."

They were meandering down the sidewalk toward Main Street to enjoy the Fourth of July parade. At least she would get to see Cody on the fire engine, and maybe after if they didn't get any calls. The engine was supposed to stop at the end of the parade route, and the Kellers were planning on allowing kids to tour the firetruck, handing out pamphlets to the parents about firework and grilling safety.

Cody had called her whenever he'd gotten a break at work, but talking on the phone wasn't the same as seeing him. Of being encircled by his strong arms while he reassured her that everything was going to be okay.

"Yeah, I'm fine." For now. Tomorrow was a different matter entirely. Tomorrow she'd be a worm on a hook. She squeezed Aaron's hand in hers and smiled down at him.

"Momma, they have flags! Can I get one?"

"Of course. Here." She reached in her pocket and pulled out two dollar bills. "Make sure you say please and thank you."

"I will." He jumped around in a quick circle, then ran for the vendor.

His level of excitement since he'd learned they were going to a parade today had been catching and was the only thing that had settled her down in between moments of sheer panic.

Aaron liked to do things for himself. He always had, but today it was too much for her to stand back and let him have a little rein. Today, she followed him closer than his shadow.

"There's Nina and Doris. Yoo-hoo! Over here." Leona pushed her glasses farther up her nose and waved frantically to the other two-thirds of the Blue-Haired Ladies who were making their way through the crowd on the busy sidewalk.

They giggled and hugged and Doris gave Aaron red lipstick kisses to his cheeks when he showed them his miniature flag.

"We have to go get on our float," Doris said through an excited grin. "This is the third year in a row we've been invited to participate in the parade."

Her ample bosoms puffed up with pride.

Rory received one back-maiming hug from Aunt Leona and promised to sit close to the curb so they could throw extra candy to Aaron.

Already, it was getting crowded on Main Street, so she staked out a small patch on the curb in front of the museum and settled Aaron in her lap. After a few minutes, a cotton candy vendor strode by, peddling his sugary wares. She bought Aaron a pink puff of the sweet treat and happily accepted delicious pinched pieces from her good little sharer as they waited for the parade to start.

Her phone chirped from her back pocket, and she answered it.

"Hey, where are you guys sitting?" Cody asked on the other line. It was hard to hear him through the commotion in the background, but just the sound of his voice settled something jumpy inside her chest.

"We're right in front of the museum," she called out.

"Is that Cody?" Aaron asked, pink sugar-drop lips smacking.

"Your son wants to say hi," she said through a grin.

"Put him on." The smile in Cody's voice threatened to melt her heart like the blob of ice cream someone had dropped on the cement beside them.

In an attempt to save her phone from little sticky fingers, she held it up against Aaron's ear and giggled as he chattered on about his flag and cotton candy. And then he regaled an intriguing tale about how a bird had pooped and the blob had landed right in front of him on the walk here. Then he described a turd he'd made in Aunt Leona's toilet this morning that looked exactly like a heart, and how it had reminded him of Cody. Rory pursed her lips to stifle her amusement at that last bit because Aaron was very serious about it. And even though Cody was likely terribly busy, he listened patiently to fecal stories and responded to everything Aaron said.

Rory loved that about him. No matter what was going on, Cody was always good at putting Aaron before whatever chaos was around him.

The fire engine blasted a honk through the phone, and a moment later, it echoed down Main Street.

"Oh!" Rory said. "Tell Cody goodbye. The parade

is about to start."

"Bye Cody! I'm saving some cotton candy for you!"

Really, there was only a paper thin layer of the treat left around the cardboard cone, but Aaron seemed intent on keeping it safe from the jostling crowd.

"We'll see you in a minute," she murmured into the phone.

"Okay. I love you, Rory Dodson."

His endearment was unexpected, and her stomach filled with happy flutters. "I love you too, Cody Keller." She hung up the phone with an uncontrolled smile stretching her face.

It took another twenty minutes for the beginning of the parade to reach them. There was an elephant float and old-fashioned cars with whacky horns. Go-karts zigzagged this way and that. The mayor rode in a convertible with Ms. Breckenridge with matching pageant waves and big smiles. The local high school band played and marched through confetti-littered streets, and a herd of miniature horses was led around by owners dressed in red, white, and blue. One of them stopped right in front of Aaron and let him pet a little bay with a fuzzy coat and pink glitter on its back. The Blue-Haired Ladies rode in a float in the shape of a coffee mug and waved from inside. They tossed ridiculous amounts of candy toward Aaron and blew him kisses, and the other kids crowded around, squealing and gathering sweets into their pockets.

Aaron hadn't stopped grinning since they'd left the house, and suddenly, Rory's heart felt too big for her chest cavity. This place was exactly where they were meant to be. They would get through this craziness with Krueger. She knew it—felt it in her gut.

She'd been right not to leave.

By the time the fire engine for Station 6 came into view, the cheers from the onlookers were borderline deafening and only added to her escalating excitement at seeing Cody.

Boone drove the engine, honking and flashing the lights, while Dade held onto the side, waving and grinning. He knocked on the window when he spotted Rory and Aaron, and Boone pulled to a stop. Cody climbed off the back and jogged toward her, clad in a navy fire department T-shirt that clung to his defined shoulders. Suspenders held up heavy looking, relaxed-fit pants with strips of reflective material. Under his helmet was a megawatt smile when he reached her. The crowd murmured around her as he approached and lifted her off her feet.

Relief slashed through his eyes. "Damn, woman. I almost forgot how beautiful you are."

She leaned down and kissed him as cheers erupted around them. Embarrassment had set her cheeks aflame by the time he set her back down.

Cody pulled Aaron up to his hip. "Can I take him on the engine? Arie and Tate are both up there with Gage."

"Can I, mommy?" Aaron was bouncing excitedly in Cody's arms, flag and cotton candy cone flapping with the motion.

Rory canted her head at Cody. "Only if you swear to protect him with your life," she said, trying for a severe look and failing.

"I will." He turned, but changed his mind and spun back around. Against her ear, he said, "Goes for you too, Rory. I'll protect you with my life." He planted a soft kiss on her cheek, and when he eased away, he had the strangest expression on his face.

Worry, where his smiled had been only moments ago.

"I know you will," she murmured, baffled at his change in mood.

He jogged back to the engine and hoisted Aaron up to Gage's waiting arms. Arie and Tate were cheering from the top and hugged Aaron as soon as he reached them. Rory giggled as her boy looked for her in the crowd. He waved as he yelled, "Hi, mommy! Look at me!"

"I see you, baby!"

Cody settled in beside his son and showed him how to toss candy on the edge of the street. He winked at her as the engine pulled away, and her cheeks flushed all over again.

After a few more floats, the parade seemed to be almost done, so she maneuvered through the milling masses, trailing the engine.

Someone bumped her from behind, and a tiny sting, like that of a wasp, pricked the back of her arm.

"Mother fluffer," she murmured, contorting her arm to try and make sure the bug was gone. A tiny drop of blood smeared across her skin when she brushed it with her finger. What the hell? She looked behind her but saw no familiar faces in the crowd, and no one seemed to be paying attention to her at all.

The hair prickled on the back of her neck as she made her way faster through the throng of onlookers. People were starting to disperse from the edge of the street now, and it was making it harder to get through the maze of bodies on the sidewalk. She was losing sight of the engine up ahead as it made its way steadily down the street. A wave of dizziness took her, and she shuffled her feet faster, bumping into a woman going the opposite direction. Rory spun and got confused. Turned around, she searched for the floats above the heads of the gathered crowd, but the town seemed to stretch and contort in front of her.

"Farfignugen," she murmured. "Farfig...nugen. That's a strange word if you say it slow."

"I'm sorry?" A man beside her said with a confused quirk to his thin brows.

"Isn't farfignugen a strange word?" she slurred, swaying on her feet and gripping his arm.

"I don't think it is a word," he said, then pried her fingers from him and ambled away.

Her head felt like it was lolling about her neck, like a planet around the sun, and she stumbled toward the side of the walkway and held onto the wall of a T-shirt shop. She was going to be sick or faint, and right now, she couldn't decide which.

Her stomach felt cold, like she'd swallowed shards of ice, and sweat dotted her forehead as she found it increasingly hard to breathe.

"Whoa, there," an older gentleman with the most alluring shade of silver hair said. He propped her upright and asked, "How much have you had to drink?"

"None." A headache was building behind her eyes, and she couldn't see straight anymore. Looking at the crowd made her feel like she was on a looping roller coaster, so instead she looked at the ground and tried to steady herself.

"Well clearly you've thrown back a little too much. Let me help you to the side so you don't get run over."

"Okay," she whispered as her tongue began to feel too swollen to talk.

The kind man escorted her to an alleyway, and as her knees began to buckle, she looked up to see Shayna opening the back of a van.

"What are you doing here?" Rory asked, locking

her knees and trying to escape the man's grip.

Shayna mimicked what she said. "God, you are all so boring. That's exactly what Cody asked yesterday." Shayna smiled a feline expression as she dragged Rory into the back of the van. "Right before he fucked me."

"Wha-what?" Rory's throat had gone dry, and her limbs weren't working anymore to fight what was happening. Cody wouldn't. He wouldn't!

The door slammed closed, and darkness descended over her. Everything was numb but her lips, and even those were beginning to tingle. As the edges of her vision blurred and shattered inward, the kind man took his place behind the steering wheel and twisted in his seat.

"Hi, Rory Dodson. It's nice to finally make your acquaintance."

Rory struggled to push air past her tightening vocal chords—struggled to keep her heavy eyelids open for a moment longer because she had to know. "Who-who are you?"

His smile was slow and empty, failing to reach his icy blue eyes. "I'm John Krueger."

FIFTEEN

Sleep pulled at Rory like the clawing mud of a swamp, but it was a noise that made her break the surface of darkness. Snarling and roaring filled the old barn that blurred before her when she tried to focus. That wasn't the noise that lifted gooseflesh across her arms, though. It was all the gunfire.

A glass of water beside her exploded, and tiny shards of glass sliced across the skin of her arm. She didn't feel it. In confusion, she stared at the welling, red slashes. A few peppered shots finished a volley before the gunfire ceased. She should be terrified, but everything felt surreal, and her body was practically floating. She must be dreaming.

But as she cleared her parched throat and

strained her eyes to focus on her surroundings, a man clad in a black, military-looking uniform, complete with helmet and bulletproof vest, ran in front of the open barn doors and into the woods beyond. Men were yelling. Some were screaming in pain. She blinked rapidly, trying to clear the mud from her mind.

"She lives," Krueger said softly from beside her. "I maybe overdid the dose, but surely you can understand. I'm used to dealing with monsters."

As the cuts in her arm began to burn, Rory looked around in terror. Against a wall of horse stalls, a long table had been set up with rows of horrifying instruments. Krueger leaned against another table, this one old and wooden as opposed to the sterile-looking plastic one that held the torture devices. His arms were crossed over his chest, his crystal blue eyes on her as if he was studying a bug or rodent. He wore a thick Teflon vest over a button-down oxford shirt.

"They aren't monsters," she said, her voice barely a hiss. "You are."

"I know a lot of good, hardworking American people who would disagree with you."

"You don't give the American public enough credit." Her throat felt like she'd swallowed gravel, and she coughed to loosen up her vocal chords.

She wasn't even tied to the rocking chair she sat in, but it didn't matter. She couldn't move her arms or legs to escape if she tried. She felt boneless.

"You are about to be a part of history," Krueger said, pushing off the table and exposing a set of tiny, black remote controls.

A quick count told her there was eight of them. Each had a number taped to it, and a red button in the center.

Krueger followed her gaze. "You're probably wondering what those are and why you're here. Rightfully so. This must be quite a detour from what you thought you'd find when you brought your son to the Breck Crew. Each operative is assigned a number." He lifted up the remote on the end. "Your mate is Operative 647."

"Don't touch that," she begged as he ran his thumb over the red button. She didn't know what it did, but she knew better than to trust a man like Krueger with a doomsday button. He seemed the type to revel in power too much.

"Would you like in on a secret?"

No. "Yes."

These little devices are what are going to help me—help us—make history. This is the control, Ms. Dodson. This is what I have that keeps shifters manageable, especially ones with the type of weapons and fight training the Kellers have." He turned his head toward the barn doors and called out, "Bring them in!"

A horde of men filed in like ants storming from a mound, but Rory was having trouble taking her eyes off the remote in Krueger's hand. When he finally set it down with a knowing smile, he said, "Focus, Ms. Dodson. I wouldn't want you to miss the show." He slid his dead glare toward the men at the other side of the room. "Cody. So glad you could join us."

With a gasp, Rory's attention snapped to the hole that was forming in the ranks. In the center, Cody, Boone, and Dade were shoved to their knees. Boone and Dade glared at Krueger with roiling hatred, but Cody's eyes were on her. Jeans clung to his bare waist, which was heaving with each breath, and a gash across his side was streaming crimson over the ridges of muscle that flexed with every exhalation.

Smears of dirt covered him and his brothers from head to toe, but Cody looked like he'd taken the worst beating out of the three of them. His face was already swelling on the right side, and a gash in his hairline made his gold-green eyes look even brighter surrounded by all that red.

"Are you okay?" His voice came out hoarse as if he hadn't used it in a long time.

She nodded, which was an improvement, because it meant she was getting feeling back. Her hands began to tingle, as if they were waking up after sleeping on them wrong. And when she looked down, her finger twitched on the arm of the rickety rocking chair. She just needed to buy them more time.

"I don't understand why you're doing this," she rasped out. "What have they ever done to you?"

"Oh, you mean besides taking the single most important thing in my life away from me? My mother died when one of those *things* tried to Turn her. Now, I'm not a stupid man, and I see the value in their abilities to further programs like this one, but surely you can see why my history with these creatures makes me a little...trigger happy. Today is different, though. Today, we're taking live specimens, which is why you are still breathing, Ms. Dodson. Congratulations on the role you've played. Science will be forever in your debt."

"Fuck science," she growled out.

Krueger frowned as if he was really taken aback. It was all an act, though. A man as empty as him couldn't be sincere if his life depended on it. "Do you know how fast they heal? Their regenerative abilities are astounding. It's what made them viable options for the missions we needed completed where survival rates were almost none. Has Cody told you everything he had to do in the war yet? If he hasn't, you've missed out. He has quite the colorful history in combat."

"What do you want, Krueger?" Cody said blandly, pulling his eyes to the silver-haired handler.

Dade canted his head and smiled. "You suck at story time, and we have shit to do."

Rage sank into the deep wrinkles on Krueger's face. "Oh, do you now? You're in a rush to be sliced up and studied? Far be it for me to keep you waiting. I only need two, though."

"Then let her go," Cody pleaded. "She's done nothing wrong."

"Goddammit, Keller," Krueger yelled explosively. "You were doing so well! How fucking predictable that you beg for her life before your own. You see, this is why your kind was doomed from the first jump in evolution that created you. This is why you are destined to fail as a species. Your survival instincts start circling the drain as soon as you find a mate. It's pathetic really." Krueger stared at the black remotes behind him and sighed as if steadying his outburst. He pulled three black remotes and sang, "Eeny meeny miney mo," to the cruel chuckles of the men with trained weapons on Cody and his brothers.

"No!" she said, clenching her fists and curling her toes. "Cody, the trackers!"

Realization slammed into her mate's hardened features the second the words left her lips. In one smooth motion, he slid a pocket knife from his jeans and gripped Boone's neck before slicing deftly. His hands moved so fast, he blurred. Boone gritted his teeth and closed his eyes as Cody shoved his finger in his neck and hooked it around something bloody and no bigger than a pain pill, and all in the span of a second. He turned to Dade as the men above them surged forward and covered them from her view completely.

Rory used every ounce of her strength to push upward and fall against Krueger, who fumbled with the controls as she slammed into his side. One fell to the ground with her, but it wasn't 647.

Desperate, she pulled up Krueger's suit pant leg and sank her teeth into his calf until she thought they'd fall from her mouth. Blood flowed against her tongue, gagging her, but she didn't care. She hadn't the strength or feeling to get up again, not yet, and this was the best she could do against the man who was trying to steal everything away from her.

Krueger screamed in pain and kicked her shoulder hard. Stars burst in her peripheral vision. "Too late!" he yelled down at her as he pushed the button on one of the remotes.

"Cody!" she shrieked.

Twin yells of agony filled the barn, but she couldn't see anything—couldn't tell if it had been her boys who were hurt. Chaos ebbed and flowed as men were knocked to the side by some unseen force.

"Don't kill the other two. I need them alive!" Krueger commanded.

Boone and Cody were up, fighting, throwing fists

as the blade flashed in Cody's hand, maiming. He slashed upward, cutting clean across a man's neck. Spinning, he elbowed another in the nose before yanking him over his shoulder and slamming him against another.

"Boone, Change!" Cody bellowed, and his brother's response was instantaneous.

Two dark-furred grizzlies exploded from them, sending waves of power and raw fury blasting across her skin. Where was Dade?

She searched the ground, and the youngest Keller lay in a crumpled heap between the bears. They were protecting him, but it wouldn't help at the rate his neck was bleeding. He held it tight, but pain creased his face, and he was gasping for breath.

"It's the acid," Krueger murmured with a chilling smile. "I've never had the opportunity to see it up close. Usually, I deactivate my pets from farther away. Each capsule can monitor their vitals, when they're mad or happy. They monitor their endorphins while they are having sex. Cody has had quite the show when he fucks you, Ms. Dodson. I can track where they are to within a few feet, and the best part of all is the kill switch. Detonate the capsule, and acid explodes outward, eroding the artery in the neck. It is laced with medicine that thins the blood and halts clotting. He'll bleed out before help can even arrive."

A sob wrenched from Rory's throat as she crawled toward him. She had to help Dade. Had to stop the red that was flowing from his throat as his brothers fought to protect him.

"Crews are so pathetic," Krueger said, following behind her. You all have this desire to make sure the others live, no matter the cost to yourself." The crack of metal on metal as he cocked a gun froze her on the grit-covered ground. His eyes narrowed with determination as his finger rested on the trigger. "I wish one of you would surprise me and try to save your own fucking life."

Shining metal sailed through the air and Cody's knife sunk deep into the space between Krueger's protective vest and his throat.

"Rory, move," Dade gritted out, crouching now and holding his neck. Red streamed between his fingers, making mud droplets on the ground beneath his feet.

Her throat clogged with terror as she scrambled toward Dade.

"Don't touch it," he rasped as she reached him. "It'll burn you."

Yanking on her shirt, she cast a baleful glance back at Krueger, who was pulling the knife Dade had thrown slowly from above his collar bone. Cody and Boone were pacing in tight circles around her and Dade, a protective barrier between them and the mercenaries with assault rifles trained. She pulled her shirt off and jammed it against Dade's neck to try and stanch the flow of blood.

A mechanical sound reverberated from the rafters above them, and Rory looked up in time to see a thick-roped net falling toward them. She screamed and covered Dade's body with her own as the heavy chords struck her in the back. The towering grizzlies above her slashed with their claws and gnashed their long canines, but it was no use. The edges had been weighted down with boulders, and the men over them used the butts of their guns to force Cody and Boone back into the center of the net.

Fear pounded through Rory as she was struck by Boone's back leg. She couldn't breathe, couldn't think. All she knew was that Dade was bleeding against her forearm and his breathing was starting to grow shallow. Something was wrong with Cody's paw. It was mangled and hanging strangely from his arm. The skin there looked chemically burned, like the injury on Dade's neck.

This was it. This was where they were going to die.

"Cody," she cried, warm tears spilling down her face as Krueger lifted his handgun toward her. This was it. This was their goodbye. "I love you."

Her mate turned toward her, eyes glassy with rage. Arching his neck against the heavy netting, he bellowed a challenging roar.

She pressed against Dade's neck with her hand. The bear she loved lurched in front of her, his fur-covered body blocking Krueger's shot. When the weapon cocked a second time, she clung to Cody's powerful leg, sobbing at how unfair it all was.

She'd only just gotten him back. She'd fallen in love for the first time, only to have what they shared mocked and ripped apart. Aaron would grow up alone. *Aaron.* Who would protect her baby now? Rory closed her eyes and inhaled the scent of Cody's fur, preparing for the inevitable blast that would rip through the man she loved.

A long, high-pitched roar rattled dust from the rafters, so loud it made Rory wince as her eardrums threatened to burst. The sound was prehistoric and electrified the fine hairs on her body.

"What the fuck was that?" Krueger yelled. A beat of silence followed before he screamed, "Take care of it!"

Cody looked back at Boone as the armed men filed out of the barn. Terror seized her as fire rain down on them the second they made it outside. A few stragglers ran back into the safety of the barn, horror written on their faces and in the whites of their eyes. Thick black smoke billowed in after them, thickening in the air until it was hard to draw a breath without choking on the fumes.

A tall man with wide shoulders strode through the smoke. His hair was dark, and his intense eyes churned gold in the muted light of the barn. Smears of ash streaked his face. He carried an ax and swung it upward in a graceful arch as one of Krueger's men ran for him. A pepper of gunfire blasted to his left, but the man ducked as if he'd expected the threat. The clicking of the attacker's empty chamber gave their rescuer enough time to leap at the man and jerk him in front of him, shielding him from another volley of gunfire.

Dade gripped the upper part of her arm and smiled at the man who fought with deadly grace.

He was as tall as a redwood and just as strong, each swing felling the few fighters that were left. A shot fired from Krueger's gun, but the man ducked easily out of the way and lifted his ax in time for the bullet to ricochet away. Arcing a look of pure hatred, he flipped the ax in his hand and chucked it. End over end it spun until it sunk deep in Krueger's vest. He blasted backward, the gun flying from his hand, and landed hard against the table with the remotes.

The dark-haired death bringer was on him before Krueger got a grip on the tiny kill switches. He yanked Krueger up and jerked his vest from his torso, then dragged him kicking and scrabbling toward the door.

The man slammed Krueger onto the ground, who rolled side to side, gasping as if the wind had been knocked clean out of him.

The man pulled the ax out of the vest and cut at the net until there was a hole large enough for the grizzlies to get through. Cody sank back into his human skin again, followed by Boone. When they were free of the net, Cody pulled her protectively against his back with his good hand.

"Who are you?" Krueger wheezed out.

"My friends call me Bruiser," the somber stranger said. "You can call me Horace Keller."

"Good to see you again, brother," Dade rasped out from his place propped up against Boone's shoulder.

"Half-brother," Bruiser said with a hard look. Turning, he nodded a small greeting to Rory and wrenched his attention back to Krueger. "Your men are all dead—proof that good shit happens to good people, and bad shit happens to bad. You're free to go."

Krueger stood uncertainly. "What do you mean?"

"I mean," Bruiser said, flipping the handle of his ax rhythmically, "I won't stop you from leaving."

"What's out there?" Krueger asked in a trembling, suspicious voice.

"The problem with you secret agencies is that you think you always have the upper hand. The tax dollars and a steady flow of intel make you feel safe. Staying hidden from the public makes you feel ahead of the game. Problem with your little program is that you stirred up shit that is better off buried, and then you brought a knife to a gun fight."

"What does that mean?" Krueger asked, straitening his spine.

Bruiser grabbed the front of his shirt and shoved him out the open door. "It means you have trackers and blackmail. We have dragons."

Enormous teeth clamped around Krueger as a blasting wind filled the barn. Rory stifled a scream and crouched to keep her balance as the legendary creature flew so low to the ground that the building shook. The dragon arched its back and aimed for the sky. Silver scales faded to an effervescent blue and then back to silver in a dazzling pattern. Giant claws pushed off the ground, blasting craters into the earth where it touched. Krueger's scream faded to nothing as the creature disappeared from the doorway. Rory ran outside with the others as the dragon caught air currents with powerful thrusts of its wings. Its tail was spiked and flowed in snakelike movements as the dragon lifted himself toward the sun.

Around them, Krueger's men lay in piles. Their final resting place was a clearing that was charred and smoldering. Smoke billowed from the ground, but there weren't any flames. Feeling ill, Rory coughed and covered her mouth.

"How the hell did you convince Damon Daye to join our cause?" Cody murmured, a deep-etched frown on the sky above.

Bruiser hooked his hands on his hips and cut a harsh look to his half-brother. "He has a vested interest in the Keller family now."

"Meaning?"

With an explosive sigh, Bruiser's eyes tightened as he watched the dragon disappear into the clouds. "Meaning I promised to marry his daughter."

SIXTEEN

Rory settled onto the porch swing Cody had erected just for her. She enjoyed reading when the weather was fair or when it was time for the boys in her life to give in to the call of their animal.

After pulling the thick blanket off the back, she stretched the soft material over her lap and curled her legs up under her. With pinks and oranges fading to gray, sunsets here were the most beautiful she'd ever seen. She'd found so much in Colorado.

Sure, the aftermath of her kidnapping had been hard. She'd been in shock for a couple of days, but a slow feeling of relief had blanketed her as time wore on and no more government agencies came for them. Cody said it was only a matter of time. He and Boone had taken video and pictures of what had been done, of the remote kill switches and incriminating evidence they found in a surveillance van that belonged to Krueger. They'd documented Dade's horrific neck burns, of which he'd barely survived. Thanks to the capsule being half way out of his throat and in Cody's hand when Krueger had detonated, the brothers had shared that burden and would don the scars of that awful day for the rest of their lives.

She'd asked Cody if his burned hand bothered him, but he'd just said, "It means my brother is alive. I'd maim the other hand, too, if it got me the same result."

That's just how Cody was, though. It's what made him a good brother and a good mate. Those tough decisions were what made him a great alpha for the Breck Crew.

He had nightmares now. He didn't talk about them much, but he'd wake with a start, sweating, chest heaving. He always held her close and would press his nose against her skin on nights like that, as if he was using her to anchor him in the present. She couldn't be certain, but likely the ghosts of the shifters he'd been forced to target were haunting him.

Shayna was in the wind and would hopefully stay that way now that her team was nothing but ashes. Rory had wondered aloud once about what happened to the IESA's bodies, but Cody had assured her Damon Daye took care of them. Just the thought of the man and all the power he harnessed dumped fear into her and got her heart to pounding. His shifter form was beautiful, but it was equally as deadly. It made her infinitely glad they'd been under his protection and not on the losing side of his wrath.

A couple of days after the battle, Bruiser had gone back to Wyoming to his beloved Ashe Crew. He'd seemed uncomfortable here and at odds with the Keller men. He'd been practically humming with relief when she'd driven him to the airport. The Breck Crew would be forever in his debt, but praise seemed to make the man fidgety.

He'd told her, "Stop thanking me. That's just what family does. They're there for each other." And when they'd needed him, and it had mattered, he had been.

Good men peppered the Keller lineage, and she was proud that Aaron would have such strong role models to look up to as he grew.

"Mommy?" Aaron asked, hesitating in the doorway.

"What is it, sweet boy?" She held her arms out so he would come snuggle her on the porch swing.

"Cody and I have something we want to give you."

His blond hair was mussed, and his shirt was nowhere to be found. Jeans clung to his narrow hips in an outfit she recognized as his shifting clothes. Cody wore the same thing when he headed out into the woods, and she smiled at how much Aaron emulated him.

"A present?"

Aaron nodded solemnly as Cody followed behind him, his shirt missing just like his son.

"Go on up in your momma's lap, boy. I want to ask you both an important question."

Rory cuddled Aaron up tight and smiled unsurely at Cody. "Fire away."

Cody knelt down on one knee, the floorboards creaking under his weight. A sharp inhalation of breath took Rory's throat as she sat up, gripping Aaron. Immediately, her eyes misted over as Cody opened a silver box he drew from his pocket. Inside, a simple gold band lined with tiny sparkling diamonds glinted in the porch light illumination.

"Oh, Cody," she breathed.

"I know we haven't talked much about me Turning you, and to be honest, I don't care if you are shifter or human. But I want my last name on you, and on Aaron. I want you to be mine in more ways than us just being bonded and mated. I want all of you, Rory Dodson. And I have no right to ask for more because you've given me something priceless already." His voice choked up, and he smiled at Aaron and rubbed his head. "You gave me our son, and then you went further and loved me despite all the muck that would've sent a lesser woman packing." Cody leaned forward and swallowed hard. "Aaron, I don't want you calling me Cody anymore. I'm your dad, and I'd be proud if you'd call me that from here on. Okay?"

Aaron grinned up at Rory, then nodded to Cody.

"And Rory," Cody murmured, his voice dipping low. "I see you hold our son when he's sleeping, and I watch your eyes soften when you are around me, and I think, I can't love her any more than in this moment right now. But then you do something else that astounds me, and I get that same breathless feeling over and over again. I get to fall in love with you every day. I'm already the luckiest man in the world that you've chosen me as your mate, but I'd be honored if you'd be my wife, too. Rory, will you marry me?"

She was already sniffling like a crybaby when she nodded and held out her hand for him to slip the ring onto. She laughed thickly as Cody scooped them both off the swing in a bear hug that made her feel safe, warm, and loved, all at once.

How could it be the man she'd met at a bar all those years ago turned out to be the one man in the world strong enough to hold her heart? He was brave, protective, and loyal and could carry the weight of the world on his shoulders and make it seem a light load. He empowered her, encouraged her, loved her with abandon or restraint. He'd taught her it was okay to lean on someone else. And watching him father Aaron had made her fall in love with him even more deeply.

Fate had a funny way of working things out. They had struggled apart and then fought to be together, but it was all worth it for this moment, right here.

A soft growl rattled Aaron's chest as she pressed kisses all over his face.

With a breathy laugh, she kissed Cody's lips.

"Yuck," Aaron groused.

Chuckling, Cody lowered Aaron to the ground, then lifted the boy's chin. Aaron looked up at him with those muddy gold eyes, a Keller trait he'd inherited from Cody along with his birthmark. "You ready to let your bear out?"

Aaron whooped and jammed his tiny fist in the air, then blasted down the porch stairs toward the yard, chest puffed out. "Bye, mommy!" he called, waving from a patch of swaying wild grass. "Daddy and me have to go do bear stuff now. Oh!" he said, doubling back a few steps. "Can you please make me chicken nuggets when I get back? And apple slices? And milk?"

"Yes, of course, since you asked so politely," she said, leaning her cheek against Cody's shoulder as he laughed at his son's food order.

Cody slid his arm around her waist and pulled her close into his side as they watched Aaron kick out of his jeans and Change into the little bear cub Rory had always protected. His Changes weren't painful anymore—not like they used to be when he'd fought the animal inside of him.

She wasn't afraid of him anymore because Cody had given their son a gift greater than any she could've ever imagined. He'd taught Aaron to keep his mind when he Changed. There were no more cages or dreading the beast. Aaron was excited and happy to shift. Anyone could see he'd blossomed here in the Colorado mountains under Cody's careful instruction and abundant adoration.

Rory inhaled deeply as her heart welled with happiness. "Will you come back to me soon?" She always asked this before he took their son to Change in the woods.

Cody smiled at the little cub who was bounding through the grass, chasing a firefly.

Every time his answer was the same.

"Always."

Want more of these characters?

Bear My Soul is the first book in a three book series called Fire Bears.

You can also read more about them in T. S. Joyce's Saw Bears series.

For more of these characters, check out these other books.

Bear the Burn
(Fire Bears, Book 2)

Bear the Heat
(Fire Bears, Book 3)

About the Author

T.S. Joyce is devoted to bringing hot shifter romances to readers. Hungry alpha males are her calling card, and the wilder the men, the more she'll make them pour their hearts out. She werebear swears there'll be no swooning heroines in her books. It takes tough-as-nails women to handle her shifters.

Experienced at handling an alpha male of her own, she lives in a tiny town, outside of a tiny city, and devotes her life to writing big stories. Foodie, wolf whisperer, ninja, thief of tiny bottles of awesome smelling hotel shampoo, nap connoisseur, movie fanatic, and zombie slayer, and most of this bio is true.

Bear Shifters? Check

Smoldering Alpha Hotness? Double Check

Sexy Scenes? Fasten up your girdles, ladies and gents, it's gonna to be a wild ride.

For more information on T. S. Joyce's work,
visit her website at
www.tsjoyce.com

Printed in Great Britain
by Amazon